"How about trial?"

"On my terms?"

"On your terms," Laurie agreed.

"And if the ninety-day trial works?"

"To the satisfaction of the three of us, then I would be willing to enter into an arranged marriage, for a four-year period."

"Fair enough. But if you feel that you want a renewal option at the end of that time, I think I could consider it."

"Don't do me any favors," Laurie Michelson said harshly as she glared at him across the desk.

"Perhaps a kiss to seal the bargain?" Harry offered.

"No thanks," Laurie muttered. "I'd sooner kiss a rattlesnake. What I'd rather see is a signed contract."

Emma Goldrick was born and raised in Puerto Rico, where she met and married her husband, Bob, a career military man. Thirty years and four children later they retired and took up nursing and teaching. In 1980 they turned to collaborative writing. After sixty years of living over half the world, and a full year of studying the Harlequin Mills & Boon style, their first submission was accepted. Between them they have written over forty books. Goldrick hobbies include grandchildren, flower gardens, reading and travel.

Sadly, in 1996, Bob Goldrick passed away. Emma continues to write in his memory.

Books by Emma Goldrick

Don't miss any of our special offers. Write to us at the following address for information on our newest releases.

Harlequin Reader Service
U.S.: 3010 Walden Ave., P.O. Box 1325, Buffalo, NY 14269
Canadian: P.O. Box 609, Fort Erie, Ont. L2A 5X3

The Ninety-Day Wife

Emma Goldrick

Harlequin Books

TORONTO • NEW YORK • LONDON
AMSTERDAM • PARIS • SYDNEY • HAMBURG
STOCKHOLM • ATHENS • TOKYO • MILAN
MADRID • WARSAW • BUDAPEST • AUCKLAND

In honor of Lt. Col. Robert N. Goldrick.
A teacher, father and coauthor in writing.
Partners to the end.

Emma

ISBN 0-373-03464-4

THE NINETY-DAY WIFE

First North American Publication 1997.

Printed in U.S.A.

CHAPTER ONE

THE cluster of aged gray wooden buildings clung high on the flank of the Appalachian Mountains, above the town of Grandell. The houses hid under the cliffs, from which a century of mining had taken the coal and the heart. The mountain leered at the town, laughing through its dozens of empty mouths, and the city cringed.

Once the houses had been clean and multi-colored and full of life. Now they were all uniformly gray, and the tired, worn forty thousand citizens, mostly unemployed, lived in a city that once sheltered eighty thousand. But a small core of determined men and women were doing their best to refurbish Grandell.

The worn hospital had the colossal nerve to call itself Grandell Teaching Hospital. Harry Mason—Dr. Harry Mason—sighed as he set a careful foot on the rotting steps of the verandah, and wondered if his five years' experience as a military surgeon hadn't all gone to waste. But jobs, even for doctors, were hard to come by, now that the massive reduction in military forces was well under way. And the Grandell Hospital was a boot-strap attempt to increase the medical strength for the future.

"Do you plan to buy that stair?" A lovely contralto voice from behind him, loaded with sarcasm. Harry looked over his shoulder. She was a slim little thing, wrapped tightly in a heavy Mackintosh raincoat. The autumn wind was nippy, rustling through the tight cap of red curls that clustered around the blue knit hat she wore. Nippy, he told himself, but not *that* cold.

"It's a wide stair," he rumbled. "You could go around." Even to himself the voice sounded threatening. Normally a smooth baritone, his head cold had dropped him into the bass range.

The girl flinched, and then bit her lip as she looked from the stair back to him. "Not on your life," she said firmly. "You must be new around here."

"Fresh off the boat," he said, chuckling. "I'm the new administrator."

She backed off one step as her face rushed to redness. "Do you know who I am?"

"No, I don't," he replied.

"Well, thank God for that," she said pertly as she squeezed around him and ran up the stairs. The screen door marked "Admissions" slammed behind her.

Harry Mason ran two fingers through his thick salt-and-pepper hair and laughed at himself. Cute, no doubt about it. Cute? Beautiful. He modified his thoughts. I'll catch up to her one of these days.

Laurie Michelson went down the main corridor at flank speed. One never ran in a hospital corridor, especially with one eye cocked over one's right shoulder. She overran the plain little door marked "Staff", and had to come back a few steps before she could dive into the room's safety. The door closed behind her with a pneumatic sigh and she leaned back against it to catch her breath. The conversation in the room stopped. A nurse and two aides concentrated on this new marvel.

"Laurie," Nurse James said. "I've never seen you rush before. Somebody after you?"

"Fate," she said softly. "Dr. Crinden told me that I'd best keep out of sight until he could explain me to the new administrator."

"And?"

"And I ran into him on the parking lot side stairs this morning!"

"Not to worry," one of the aides commented. "I knew his mother. She said he's as amiable as a—"

"Yeah," Laurie said. "As amiable as a black bear. I saw the size of his teeth. Perhaps he thought he was showing his good nature, but it looked to me as if he was searching for a place to bite. I suppose he loved his mother. Most of these big male terrorists have that sort of attachment."

"You might be right," Nurse James reflected solemnly, hiding the teasing gleam in her eyes. "I'm just relating what his mother told me, a long time ago." She paused for reflection. "But she's dead, you know."

Laurie Michelson, thirty-two years old, still as naïve as a girl could be, shuddered and struggled out of her winter coat. "I really need this job," she said mournfully.

"You've got a whole year of university left?" Nurse James asked.

"Six additional credits after this semester," Laurie admitted. "I have two semesters to go and I need the money."

The electric clock-alarm on the wall buzzed.

"Day shift," the nurse announced, and she, and her two aides, swept out into the hall. As soon as the staff-room door closed behind them, they broke out in giggles. Teasing Laurie Michelson was one of the few delights left in the almost bankrupt hospital. And she was so easily teased.

Laurie paced the long narrow room twice, then dropped into a comfortable chair. The green wall paint soothed her. She fumbled in her shoulder bag for a cigarette, without luck. With shaking fingers she dumped the contents of the bag out onto the low coffee table. Everything in her bag had a purpose; at the moment she just couldn't remember what that purpose might be.

In a far corner of the mess was a rumpled cigarette. She picked it up, disgusted. She had quit smoking four times this year, and it was only September. Footsteps thundered down the corridor outside the door—and went past.

Laurie crumbled up the cigarette and threw the remnants into the waste basket. Not for anything was she going to break her vow against smoking. Well, not at this particular moment. But the footsteps had shaken her, disturbed her minuscule pot of bravery. She took a deep breath, stood up, and headed for her locker in the far corner.

Her uniform needed cleaning. Much to her surprise the diagnostics department had called on her services with considerable frequency lately. All this from a department that had once claimed her idea as pure idiocy. She was grinning as she slipped into her uniform: a pair of cuddly pink flannel two-piece pajamas and slippers to match, with little red tassels on the toes. The hospital robe which covered it was deadly dull green. She slipped into it with a little moue of disgust.

Her schedule hung on a clipboard on the wall. She checked the day's requirement and the usual dialogues. Three appearances—two for beginning four-man residents. One appearance for a group of three would-be nurse-practitioners.

Laurie groaned at that one. The nurses were hard to fool. Another wall buzzer sounded. She checked her watch, shrugged, tucked her script inside her robe, and headed for the examination room.

Dr. Harry Mason moved along so rapidly that the head nurse had difficulty keeping up. The good doctor was displeased with his inspection. Nurse Hart had only to look at the thunderclouds on his brow to know. Not that she was perturbed. At sixty-three, two years away from retirement, Alison Hart knew all there was to know about Grandell Hospital, and where all the bodies were buried, so to speak.

"And what's in here?" he asked grumpily.

"That's one of the classrooms," she said. "Diagnostics. A practicum. A basic course."

He almost passed it by. It was getting close to lunchtime and he could smell something good wafting down the hall. But he was a man of duty, nothing less.

"Practicum? How the hell do you practise a diagnostic?" He nodded at the door. She shrugged and opened it. Doctors didn't open doors if there were others available to do so. Not even in practically bankrupt hospitals.

He brushed by her and took a seat in the rear of the room. "Ah," he said softly. The girl who had dodged him on the outside stairs was leaning against a corner of the teacher's desk—dressed in pajamas?

So that's where I made my mistake, he thought. A patient, not an employee! He leaned back in his chair to listen, barely noticing the broad grin on Nurse Hart's face. The lecture room was arranged as a circular pit. Down on the floor four students and one instructor were gathered around a desk.

"Just how do you feel?" The student doctor had seen the new administrator come in, and he flushed a little, attempting to put on a show.

"Feel?" Laurie used her best worn-out voice. "Oh, I feel tired. All the time tired. I ain't but nineteen years old, and I'm all the time tired. Maw says it's just bein' lazy, but I ain't, ya know. Tired."

"Tired," the student reflected as he scribbled on the chart attached to his clipboard.

"Yeah, tired," Laurie repeated.

"Anything else?" The older student stared at her suspiciously.

"Thirsty," Laurie said. "I drink like a fool. Water, you know. My mouth is always dry. I hafta run to the bathroom all the time." She wiggled into a different position against the desk. "All night long, runnin' to the bathroom. Awful, ya know?"

They all nodded. Dr. Mason chuckled and extended his feet under the row of chairs in front of him.

There was a moment of quiet. "Are there any other questions? Any other tests?" the instructor asked.

"I'd like to check her vital signs—and listen to her heart," the third student said. "Turn around, miss."

"That young man was a medical corpsman in the Marine Reserves," Nurse Hart whispered. Mason nodded.

"Unbutton your pajama top, please."

"Unbutton my—what?"

"Unbutton your pajamas, please. I want to listen to your heart."

Laurie reluctantly complied, looking over her shoulder at him as he pulled her top up and applied his stethoscope to the middle of her back.

"Take a deep breath and hold it," he commanded.

She squealed. "Cold," she complained. It wasn't in the script, but from time to time she liked to vary the lines.

"Deep breath," the student commanded sternly. Laurie giggled and complied. "And exhale."

"I guess it ain't important, you bein' a doctor and all," she said, and squealed again as the instrument touched down at another point.

"Deep breath," he commanded. "And exhale. Turn around please, and—"

"Now just a darn minute," Laurie huffed. "You ain't gonna put that thing on my—"

"All necessary if you want to get better."

Laurie sighed and turned slowly, closing her eyes as he tried to get more readings. Now the student seemed more embarrassed than Laurie as he pulled the pajama top up and traced a line under and between Laurie's firm, sizable breasts. Dr. Mason jumped, and then settled down again. His own actions bothered him. Doctors of necessity had to touch bare flesh. So why should this little bit of clumsiness upset him? He shifted uneasily in his narrow chair as the student quickly withdrew. Laurie managed to re-button her pajamas and settle her pajama top.

"Any more tests or readings?" the instructor asked. "In that case you are required to make a list of any lab readings you might require, and your possible diagnosis."

"I'd like to see those preliminary diagnoses," Dr. Mason murmured.

"I'll bring the papers to you as soon as the instructor has checked them off. Shall we go?" Nurse Hart asked.

Harry Mason had a little problem untangling his feet in the narrow row. The head nurse blinked a quick look at his semi-dazed face, and recognized the symptoms. She put a hand on his arm as if to guide him, and steered him out into the hall.

Down in the pit of the classroom the four students shook their heads and took their best guesses. The instructor collected their papers. Laurie Michelson tightened the belt on her pajamas, struggled into her hospital robe, and checked her wristwatch. She had two more classes left before her drama class down at the university in the center of Grandell, and she had been late three times this month already.

She raised an eyebrow to the instructor when they were all finished. He nodded. Ignoring the students, she climbed up out of the pit and went out into the hall. Dr. Mason was chatting with the head nurse, standing by the front door.

Laurie had been working at this job for six months, and was accustomed to the hospital's routine. But this tall, lean man bothered her. Embarrassed her, for a fact. Besides, she hadn't time to change back into her street clothes. Not that that mattered back at the university, where the drama department spent more than a little time teaching its students how to disguise themselves. But here, under the eye of the administrator? And her mother the doyenne of society in Grandell?

Laurie gulped, licked her lips, and started down the hall at full speed. Nurse Hart turned and went off down the corridor to the office wing. But Laurie had caught the doctor's eye.

"Miss," he called, and offered his best smile. Laurie Michelson managed to avoid him and his smile, and turned left toward the staffroom. There was no time to dress. She shrugged into her heavy coat, picked up her remaining clothing, and went back out the door like an Olympic runner doing the hundred-yard dash. Dr. Harry Mason was still standing idly by the big swinging doors.

"Young lady," he said in his best commander's voice. "We don't run—" And by that time she was halfway through the outer doors. His voice dropped to a conversational level. "We don't run in the hospital corridors." He shook his head at the back of her and muttered, "I must be getting old."

"Me too," she called back at him as she slipped by him and hurried down the rickety stairs.

"Just a darn minute," he called after her. The wind whistled around the corner of the hospital, spraying her with the red-gold of maple leaves. She shrugged her coat more closely around her. Her bra fell out of the bundle of clothing tucked under her right arm.

"Hey, stop!"

"In a pig's eye," she muttered to herself as she swooped downward to snatch up the bra, and then increased her speed.

There was a pay-telephone booth in the lobby of the arts building at the university downtown. She stepped into it and slid the door shut just in time. A pair of rushing male freshmen shouldered their way up to the door and rapped on the glass. She ignored them with the cool disdain of a senior class member, and fumbled in her purse for change. Three rings and her mother answered.

"I'm at the university," she said. The pair of freshmen knocked at the door again. She slid the door partway open. "Get lost," she commanded. "This phone is reserved for seniors." And then turned back to the instrument.

"No, not you, Mom. You left a note at the hospital for me to call you. What's up?"

"Something I had entirely forgotten," her mother told her. It was no surprise to Laurie. Her mother was running close onto sixty-five years old, and forgetting was one of the things she did really well. "There's a little welcoming get-together at the country club. Six o'clock cocktails and then dinner."

"No problem," Laurie said. "Whom are we honoring?"

"I—ah—don't seem to remember," her mother said. "Somebody new in town—from the— No, I just don't remember. Somebody important, I'm sure."

"I'm sure he must be," Laurie said. "Or she. Not to worry, love. I'll be home by four-thirty, and we'll just bomb right out to the club in our glad rags, and honor the devil out of him. Or her."

"Yes," her mother agreed, momentarily distracted from her multitude of problems. "Bomb right out? Not in that car of yours! Every time I ride in that car I panic!"

"It's not the car," Laurie lied, "it's my driving."

"Oh, well, in that case…" Her mother sighed and put down the handset. Laurie did the same and pushed her way out of the booth, her bundle of clothing trailing behind her.

"And don't let it happen again," she admonished the two freshmen as she dashed by them, heading for the elevator.

"Hey, lady," the taller one called after her. "You dropped your—"

Laurie turned around. "My bra. You can't play on the football team if you don't know the names." The shorter man ran over, carrying her dropped articles, and choked on an apology. The elevator door opened behind her and Laurie backed in.

"And don't believe anything a senior tells you," she called out at them as the door closed. And then added to herself, Especially a senior!

Laurie sat through two hours of classes, bored almost to tears. With two years behind her in community theater she had discovered the truth behind an old adage: Those who can, do. Those who can't, teach. But the magic words in today's world were "Get a degree," and the words behind those were "class credits." So she labored in the vineyard, daily hoping that the grapes would not *all* be sour. She dreamed a little between the lecturer's exclamation points. About Dr. Mason—large, dependable Dr. Harry Mason.

When a girl had a hankering for marriage and a baby or two, solid, dependable men were hard to find. Long ago she had discarded the good-looking part of the equation, substituting employed instead. And who could be better employed than a doctor? Not that Harry Mason was homely, mind you. But he had lived a good many years in the military, a profession that was noted for damage and destruction. She wondered exactly how many years.

She was so determined to find out that when the buzzer rang, signaling the end of the class, she sat still, dreaming, while her classmates tumbled out into the hall, chattering away about their own Dr. Masons. And since that was pure poppycock—there couldn't be twenty-six of him, could there?—she snapped out of her fantasies and struggled down to the parking lot and her ten-year-old car. Which brought her home to the outskirts of town—almost, in fact, out of town—at just four-thirty, as promised.

"Just in time," her mother greeted her. "Hurry up and change."

"Hurry up? For drinks at six?"

"Well, we wouldn't want to be late, would we?"

Laurie shook her head and then grinned. Her father, who had been a great big drink of water, had always referred to her mother as Mrs. Featherbrain—but with deep affection. Both the Michelson ladies missed him, but four years was a long time dead, and memories had long since faded around the edges.

It was a big house, half paid for before her father died, with more closet space than clothes. He had scrupulously made the mortgage payments for the house. Well, half of them, anyway, and as a result had left nothing else behind him, except for Mrs. Michelson's insurance fund.

It was enough to feed them, but her mother had never forgotten her salad days in high society and spent as if she had inherited the Duchy of Lancaster. And that left nothing for Laurie's education or clothes. A Cinderella situation, minus the Fairy Godmother. So Laurie paid most of the bills from her miscellaneous jobs, and her mother paid the mortgage monthly from his insurance.

Laurie was never one for feeling sorry for herself. Since high school days she had found odd jobs, part-time jobs, summer jobs, years of baby-sitting, occasional modeling jobs at a local boutique. All of which, combined with her scholarships, had carried her through three years of college. Three years and four months, to be exact, searching for a piece of paper signifying her degree, or Prince Charming, or both or whichever came first. If there were such a fellow.

There were two dresses hanging in her closet. One a basic black that was perhaps just a smidgen too tight around the hips, the other a solid brown with a low boat collar that was, in the conservative southern mountains of Tennessee, just a touch *too* modern for comfort. Laurie flipped a mental coin; the black won. It was either wear it without a slip or tear the seams out. She dressed cautiously and brushed her hair.

That was the easy part. Twenty strokes with a brush and her curls snapped back into tight little ringlets, and would not be budged, except perhaps by a tropical rainstorm.

Her mother was waiting for her in the living room, with her usual drink in one hand and a large, official-looking envelope in the other. "Ready, my dear?"

Laurie collapsed into an elderly stuffed chair, and consulted her wristwatch. "Ready, but we have an hour to spend, Mother. What's in the envelope?"

"Oh, nothing important." For the first time in years Laurie saw her mother blush. Unusual, she thought. "Something from the bank, dear. They keep sending me these things every month."

"But you don't want to buy any?"

"No. They are so persistent. Stand there by the door," her mother directed.

Laurie got up slowly, already worn out from the day's frenetic activity. The sun, normally cut off by the tail end of the mountain range, had managed to penetrate Culver Gap, and when Laurie stepped into the open doorway it silhouetted her.

"Oh, my dear, you can't wear that!"

"It's not a question of can't," Laurie said. "That's all there is."

"But I can see you right through—at least wear something underneath."

"I can't, Mother. There's not enough room for me and 'something underneath'. And my other dress is too—open at the top. It's either this or I'll have to stay home. You could always go without me. And I could use the rest." For the first time in years Laurie was on the ragged edge, and unwilling to jump. Her mother fluttered and then gave up.

"No, I can't go without you. Everyone would talk. We'll just have to hope—you'll just have to not stand in front of any lights, my love. Lord, pressures, pressures, pressures. I don't know how I put up with them. I believe I'll take a little nap."

Laurie settled back into her chair and watched as her mother walked out of the room. She's old, she told herself. You have to make allowances. Her father raised her to be a lady, a Southern Belle, and she doesn't know anything else.

"What I really have to do," Laurie muttered, "is resign from all this high society and find friends who'll accept me for what I am. And just think what Mother would say about that!"

The Michelson ladies arrived just before six o'clock, Laurie's old car gasping as it climbed the slight hill to the golf course. There were a dozen or more cars parked outside the clubhouse. "More than the last meeting," Mrs. Michelson said. "Maybe there's something to this bootstrap business. Establish the upper crust, and the town will rise to it."

"Oh, Mom. Three quarters of the town are coal miners. Are you suggesting they join?"

"Nonsense, girl. I don't know where you get these crazy ideas. Coal miners' wives in the country club? Preposterous."

"Democracy," Laurie amended. "That's what it's called. Do the town a world of good, it would. During World War II didn't all the women join the club and welcome?"

"Yes, but that was different, dear, and a terribly long time ago. Why, I was just a girl in those days. Enough of that. There's a goodly crowd inside. Let's go in."

So, led in by the nose, so to speak, Laurie Michelson

followed her mother inside the gingerbread construction that had served Grandell for more years than many of its neighbors had lived. The reception room had served as a basketball court during the 1980 depression years. A few bedraggled sets of bunting hung from the arched roof. A few tables had been gathered together on a narrow platform, signifying a dais—a place for the leaders to plume themselves.

As they moved across the room, Mrs. Michelson kept introducing her daughter, as if it were her first appearance in society, rather than her three hundredth. Laurie took it all in good humor, and hoped things would get better almost immediately. Which they didn't.

"I must present you to Hans Depner—he's here." Laurie's head came up with a start. Not Hans! It was too late to stop her mother. She was well and truly hooked!

"Mother," Laurie whispered urgently. "You *knew* he would be here. I'm never going to forgive you for this. Never."

"It was a silly misunderstanding," Mrs. Michelson maintained stoutly. "Boys will be boys. One expects that. I'm sure he treated you like a lady!"

"Lady, hell!" her daughter snapped. "He practically tried to rape me. If it hadn't been for Max, the night watchman, he might easily have succeeded."

"Now, now, Laurie, it couldn't have been all that serious. His mother is the chairwoman of the ladies' auxiliary. The Depners have been pillars of our community since the beginning of the century. Now don't make a scene."

"If that man comes near me I'll make such a scene as you've never seen before—right in the middle of the floor."

"Well, if that's the way you're going to act, we might as well go home," the dowager said huffily. "It's no way for a lady to act. Your father would be shocked beyond reason!''

''Roll over in his grave, I'll bet,'' Laurie added. Her mother glared at her, and by that time Hans Depner had come close enough to make his bows.

''Mrs. Michelson, Miss Laurie—it's been a long time since I've had the pleasure of your company.''

''And it will be a long time before it happens again. I have a long memory, Mr. Depner. A very long memory.''

''Are you suggesting that I did something out of the ordinary?'' he asked pleasantly.

''Bingo,'' she said forcefully. ''Attempted rape is considered beyond the pale, Mr. Depner.''

''Perhaps you might like to discuss this with me, Mr. Depner.'' Laurie whirled around, startled. Dr. Harry Mason—all one hundred and eighty pounds of him. All five feet ten inches and over of him, offering Hans Depner a choice of death in the late afternoon.

''Oh, really,'' Mrs. Michelson interjected. ''Not here in the club. Hans Depner is the son of the county clerk. People already speak of him as the next county registrar, a political plum where little work brings a handsome income.''

Mothers with unattached daughters considered him to be a fine catch. Mothers such as Mrs. Michelson, whose flighty concerns had nothing to do with her daughter's happiness, thought Laurie.

''I'm not much concerned about where and how,'' the good doctor declared. ''Just about when and why.''

And that, Laurie Michelson told herself, is a whole bunch of good news. This is a man who— And her mind whirled around like a computer hard disk, listing all the dozens of reasons why Dr. Harry Mason was a damnably good man to have around.

But Hans Depner had a considerable concern for his neat nose, and felt it threatened. He backed off a step or two and held up both hands in abject surrender. "Look," he said. "I'm in the market for a conversation, not an assault. You're the new doctor, aren't you?"

Mason nodded.

"I certainly wouldn't want to do anything nasty to your face. It might scare off the customers," Depner said.

"That's kind of you," Mason said. "Only I'm a surgeon. You ought to worry about my hands. Fragile, you know. So now, if you would just apologize to the young lady and then go away, everything would be just fine. Right?"

Red-faced, deciding the better part of valor was to give in, Depner complied.

"Doctor?" Laurie's mother could be swayed. A surgeon in the hand was worth two county registrars in the bush. She nudged her errant daughter.

"Dr. Mason," Laurie supplied. "My mother, Mrs. Michelson."

"Harry," the doctor said, extending a hand.

"Maybelle," Mrs. Michelson returned, taking the offered hand. "A surgeon. How exciting. My late husband was in the medical profession as well. A pharmacist, you know. We owned the largest pharmacy in Grandell."

The doctor nodded in recognition; birds of a feather, he seemed to indicate. Team members, so to speak. Maybelle Michelson blushed, and, had she been forty years younger, would have curtsied. Laurie blushed as well. For herself *and* her mother, and prayed that the roof of the old building might not collapse. It didn't.

Laurie was nursing a ginger ale in her hand. Prepared with infinite skill by the elderly bartender to look like a whiskey and soda, iced to perfection, and just what she needed at that embarrassing moment.

"Dear Lord, what are you doing?" Dr. Mason snatched at her glass, but it had sweated down its sides, and his hand slipped. Laurie added another hand around it, and struggled to get the cool liquid to her mouth. Almost in desperation the doctor swung a flat palm at the glass and at her, and knocked the drink off to the floor, where it shattered.

Shards of glass bounced and scattered. The ice cubes broke up into tiny splinters and joined the confusion. Mrs. Michelson turned pale and almost fainted.

Laurie, caught between two emotions, grabbed at her mother and glared at Harry Mason. "Oh, my," Mrs. Michelson said as she gasped for breath.

"Just what the hell are you trying to do?" Laurie muttered.

"Stupid," the doctor roared. His quarterdeck voice overrode all the conversations in the room. Silence pounded in and seized control. Mrs. Michelson hardly knew what to say. She looked meekly at the doctor.

"Your daughter," he said in a steel-like voice, "came into the hospital today and was plainly diagnosed as a diabetic. And now you let her drink alcohol? Stupid!"

"She what? Diabetes? No Michelson would ever have that. Only poor people—"

"Which we are," Laurie interrupted. "There's hardly anyone in town who's poorer than we are."

"Nonsense, Laurie Lee. Maybe the man is right. Stupid! I told you and I told you, don't be messin' around with those people down on South Water Street."

"Mother, you are about as batty as he is. You don't catch diabetes by going down to South Water Street. It's not an infectious disease you catch from poor people. And as for you, *Dr.* Mason, if that's the way you diagnose patients in the hospital the cause is lost. I did *not* come to the hospital to be diagnosed. I mean—I did, but not the way you think." She whirled away from him and headed for the door.

"Laurie," her mother called feebly. And then she turned to the doctor. He was, after all, a man of authority—a surgeon. "Now see what you've done," she moaned as she searched for a handkerchief which ought to have been in her purse. Ought to have been, but wasn't.

"What have I done now?" Mason asked belligerently.

"How do I know?" Maybelle Michelson said, crying into the handkerchief he'd offered. "But somebody did something. My baby never, ever acted like that before! Never!"

"Yes, I see that," Harry Mason said, sighing. "I wish I understood women!"

CHAPTER TWO

"WELL, what do you have to say?"

The four students shifted uneasily in the circle of chairs arranged facing the battered desk of the new administrator, whose face looked as battered as the desk. But none of them offered an opinion.

"It can't be that difficult," Dr. Mason said. "All four of you conducted the interview. All four of you made copious notes. All four of you submitted a written tentative diagnosis. Now who was supposed to inform the patient?"

The former marine, older and smaller than the others, raised a hand. "Felder," he identified himself. "None of us were supposed to tell the patient until the lab reports came back. When they did, there was nothing to tell."

"What?"

"All of us asked for a blood sugar test. It came back from the lab, and I asked for a recheck."

"And what was the reading?"

"Eighty-six," Felder reported hesitantly. "Tested three times. After she had a big breakfast. Eighty-six. I went down to watch the third test. Everything appeared to be quite correct. The conclusion is that whatever she had it wasn't diabetes!"

Harry Mason scratched at the side of his chin. He had gone from the evening's social event directly to the hospital, where a four-car accident had stacked up patients in the tiny emergency room, leaving him no time for either shave or shower. And that, he assured himself, had to stop. Living in Grandell was something on the order of running a battlefield hospital.

He waved all the students toward the door, threatening them with a mumbled apology. They disappeared like chaff fluttering down the breeze and then he sat back in his chair to think.

Somewhere out in his hospital there was some kind of small magic going on and he, by damn, meant to put an end to it. His in-box was stuffed with papers to be signed. He dumped them all out on the blotter in front of him. After this, he thought, and then I'll go find that— that—person. He reached for his pen and set to work.

What with three interruptions for emergency consultations, and one operation, also an emergency, it was well past three in the afternoon before he cleared his desk and felt free to prowl the corridors of his decrepit domain.

Laurie Michelson had reported for work fifteen minutes early. For a non-drinking Methodist she had a surprisingly large headache. Her mother had jawed and jawed all the way home, from the depths of the back seat.

"What a marvelous man," she'd said. "And a doctor, too. How could you possibly have been rude to such a fine man? You could have married him within the week. On his salary we could have had the roof repaired, the porch painted, the cesspool cleaned— Lord, girl, what kind of a fool are you?"

"If that's what you want, Mother, you could marry him yourself! I can't believe you'd want me to steal such a prize away from you," Laurie had replied angrily. "Such a big man, well-built, employed—what more could you ask?"

"You don't understand," her mother had said, shivering in anguish. "Thirty years ago I would have jumped at the chance. But now... He's so—big. You're too young to understand what that means. A girl your size, your age—you could have handled him with no trouble at all!''

And so on, through half the night, until Laurie, her back to the wall, had snarled, "I'm not looking to enlist as a brood mare,'' and stomped out of the room.

All of which were the causes of the early-morning report, and the massive headache. And when she sneaked in the back door of the hospital and pussy-footed down the corridor to the staffroom there were the same nurse and her two aides of the morning shift, none of whom had ever been invited to a ball at the country club, and were eager to hear all the little details.

"No, I did *not* have a good time,'' Laurie said grumpily. "No, I did *not* dance with Dr. Mason. And no, I didn't—do anything at all!''

"A likely story,'' Nurse said. "Didn't do anything?''

"Didn't do anything!'' Laurie insisted as she opened her locker, checked her clothing requirements, and read her instructions for the day. And groaned.

"Now what's the matter?'' the nurse asked.

"Incomplete instructions,'' Laurie muttered. "I'm supposed to have phlebitis, and I haven't the slightest idea what the symptoms are.''

"That's an easy one,'' the nurse said. "Blood clotting, usually in the leg. A sharp pain behind the major muscles, your leg aches, you're warm. If the clot breaks loose it's goodbye Laurie. It could be carried to the heart, and that would be that—probably.''

"Oh, my,'' Laurie said. Her headache felt worse than it had a few minutes previously. "It couldn't just be a headache?''

"Not usually,'' Nurse said. "Don't try to make your symptoms worse than they need to be. You're a standardized patient, and the students are not anywhere near graduation. KISS.''

"KISS? I—not with students. I don't even know them."

The buzzer on the wall clock went off. "KISS," Nurse said. "The hospital motto. Keep It Simple, Stupid." And all three of the morning team rushed for the door and their assigned ward duties.

"Easy enough for you to say," Laurie muttered as she changed out of her trousers and into the required skirt. "I suppose you'd want me to KISS Dr. Mason?" She shuddered. The idea scared her half to death. And yet there was a delicious little taste behind it all.

The buzzer rang again, signaling the start of classes. Late as usual, Laurie mussed up her hair, re-buttoned her blouse crookedly, and pulled a corner of the blouse loose from the skirt to add a little sloppiness to her costume.

She peered out of the slightly opened door into the corridor, looked cautiously up and down the hall, saw nobody, and dashed for room two twenty-six, where the class was scheduled. Before opening the door, she crammed a couple of sticks of gum into her mouth and chewed mightily. Then she yanked the door open and limped down into the pit of the classroom.

"Three minutes late," the nurse-instructor murmured.

"Couldn't help it," Laurie returned loudly. "I got this pain in my leg, see. I hafta limp, ya know. I could not of gone no faster! I bin hot and cold the last couple of days."

"Ah. Pain in your leg? Gentlemen." The other woman waved the four male students forward and the inquisition began.

Their diagnoses took all the morning and half the afternoon, until one of them stumbled on the magic word. And yelled it at the top of his voice. "Phlebitis!" The other three students groaned. "It was so obvious," Felder said. "We could have guessed it by the middle of the morning. Now what?"

"The treatment is not required," the nurse-instructor said. "But, just in case you run into something like this in the future, you've diagnosed a dangerous problem. Miss Laurie has a blood clot in her leg. If it breaks loose and reaches her heart we have a very serious problem. The prescribed treatment is a series of blood-thinning shots to dissolve the clot and restore normal circulation."

"Like a Sherlock Holmes mystery," one of the students declared. "Once you've got all the clues it becomes simple to put a name to it."

"Don't forget we've missed our lunch, and it's darn near to supper," another said.

"There'll be something available in the kitchen," one of the third-year men remarked. "And we ought to invite Laurie to come along for a snack as well."

From a covey of serious would-be doctors they turned into a mob intent on food-stealing. And Laurie, as hungry as all the rest, followed them along back down to the basement and into the preserve of the chief cook, whom neither the chief administrator nor the head nurse could command. But unfortunately the administrator had also missed his lunch, and was occupying a seat on the very first bench of the very first table. And all the enthusiastic noises ran out of their lungs, to be superseded by a deadly silence.

Dr. Mason rose from his seat and waved them all onto the benches. "Do I understand you've made a successful diagnosis, gentlemen?"

"Unanimous decision," the nurse-instructor reported. "Of course they took well over three hours to reach that conclusion."

Waiters began to fill the table spaces with food, and the conversation became general. Until the administrator stood up and made another announcement. "Of course four unanimous decisions can all be wrong. You don't run a hospital by majority rule, you know." And then his eye caught Laurie, trying her best to hide in the last seat at the table.

"Ah. Miss Michelson. This is the girl who was almost at death's door yesterday with a case of diabetes. Not so?"

A concerted groan rose along with the smoke from the succulent beef stew.

"Well, I don't care," Felder said. "I haven't had a bite to eat since six this morning!"

"Go ahead, dig in," Dr. Mason instructed. "Feed the hungry healers, while Miss Laurie and I have a short conversation. Miss Laurie?"

With a sigh Laurie gave up her position and stood up. The doctor was still conversing with the student nearest him. Desperate for some food, Laurie stole the ladle from the bowl, dipped and filled it, and blew on it for cooling purposes all the time Dr. Mason was talking. And when he stopped talking she jammed as much of the stew down her throat as she might hold. The Michelson mouth was not quite big enough.

"You needn't choke yourself," the doctor advised as he guided her to his office and closed the door behind her. Laurie backed cautiously away from him.

"Sit," he commanded, and pulled out a chair for her.

Laurie hesitated for a moment, and then slipped into the chair. "I am not," she announced firmly, "an employee of this hospital." Having proven her courage, she folded her hands to quiet their quivering, and set her fists up on the table top.

"Are you not, now?" he murmured. "And would you guess, young lady, that what I want to find out is—just what is your relationship to my hospital?"

Oh, Lord, Laurie thought, *his hospital?* The imperial ownership? And if I tell him the truth he'll blow his stack and I'll be out on the street with seven months to go before graduation! Yes, her conscience agreed. And if I don't tell him the truth I'll be out on the street a lot sooner than that, and—

She sighed.

"I am an actress," she started out, "working on contract with the hospital."

"And what the devil do I need an actress for on my staff?" he demanded.

"I play the part of a standardized patient," she managed to whisper.

"Speak up," he roared.

Laurie blocked her ears and shuddered. Nothing affected her more than loud mouths. Especially loud mouths being operated by massive angry men. She took a deep breath and leaned toward him. "Shut up," she said firmly.

And he did. He closed his mouth tightly, chewed on his lower lip, seemed to be counting to ten—or one hundred as the case might be—and then gave her a grim sort of executioner's smile. "Tell me all about it," he said softly. "Standardized patients?"

"Yes." She rearranged herself in the chair, smoothed down her skirt, and mustered up some courage. "When I was up at school in Boston," she said, "I answered a casting call—much to my surprise—at Deaconess Hospital. They, and several other Boston hospitals, are affiliated with Harvard Medical School.

"It appeared that students were having trouble with textbook descriptions of some common ailments. And questioning the patients themselves many times brought out the wrong answers and left the patients frustrated. So somebody came up with the idea of hiring actors to state the cases. Now a good many schools throughout the nation have adopted the scheme, and we are known as standardized patients."

"Well, I'll be..." he said.

"Probably," she answered pertly.

He glared at her. "And we pay you for this—service?"

"You do. Not what it's worth, but beggars can't be—"

He waved her comment off, tapped his fingers on his desk for a few concentrated seconds, then pushed his chair back and came to his feet.

"And yet you and your mother are members of the country club?"

"My father bought each of us a lifetime membership," she murmured. "It was a lot cheaper in those days. Would you believe I can sport it up at the country club, but I can't afford to buy a meal there—or a drink, for that matter? I suppose you've heard about the New Rich? Well, my mother and I are leaders of the New Poor! And now I expect you're going to cancel my contract?"

She came to her feet and confronted him. A tiny tear rolled down her cheek. She sniffed it away and glared back at him.

"Lord, no," he growled at her. "Your contract will be renewed. It's a hell of a good idea!" And then, before she could catch her breath, he asked, "I don't suppose you do other little jobs?" He whipped out a massive handkerchief from his pocket and wiped her tear away.

"Anything," she said, gulping. "Well, almost anything. Just so long as it's moral and decent and legal—anything!"

"Then I have a problem that might interest you," he said as he sat down again. "A personal problem which I hope you might work in among your hospital appearances."

"I'm willing to consider anything, but my time is limited. My schooling—at the university—"

"Drama?"

"Yes. I need six more credits in January to graduate."

"And how about your acting at the hospital? You can't get credits for that?"

"I—I don't think so. I have this tough advisor who thinks nothing is worthwhile if it's not earned under the university roof."

He clasped his hands over his flat stomach and rocked a couple of times in his chair. "This advisor—does he ever get sick?"

Laurie giggled. "I don't *think* so, but he's always complaining about his stomach. He takes at least one day off every two weeks because of his stomach problems."

"You wouldn't mind if I talked to him about your credits—and his stomach problems?"

Laurie's eyes lit up, and a grin added more than a little to her beauty, he thought. Why hadn't he thought of that before? Her beauty, that was. Separately, her various attractions were losers; her eyes were too big, her nose tended to point upward, and one of her front teeth was ever so slightly chipped. But measured all together she had a certain gamine charm that no man could possibly overlook.

"No," she said, "I wouldn't mind at all. A girl my age needs all the help she can get. But within the limits of my time, what can I do for you?"

Harry Mason took a deep breath, trying to settle his nerves. This was the critical point.

"You may not know, but I've been married..."

"Oh," she said cautiously. But of course I should have expected that, she thought. He's a handsome man. Not so young, of course. It takes a long time for a man to get a medical degree, and then he was in the military, and— "I've *been* married?" Meaning he isn't married now? A little chill ran up her spine. She hadn't thought of a man in that relationship for years!

He cleared his throat. She stopped daydreaming, composed herself, and looked up at him. "No," she said. "I don't know anything about you, except that you're a surgeon.''

"Yes," he said, and then pondered. "It takes a long time. How old would you think I am?"

"I haven't the slightest idea," Laurie said. "Thirty four—thirty five?"

"Well, that's kind of you." And he smiled for the first time. "How about thirty-seven? Does that bother you?"

"Bother me?" Laurie shifted in her chair. A woman should never tell her— Why not? "Actually I'm thirty-two myself. Why would thirty-seven bother me? My family doctor is almost seventy."

"Ah." He rocked in his chair again. "Then you're not bothered by—elderly affairs?"

Laurie shook her head, almost giggling. "Elderly affairs are like my mother's generation. She's sixty five."

"I'm not married any more."

"Oh? Your wife died?"

"Not exactly."

"Not exactly?"

"And I have a nine-year-old daughter."

So why is he telling me all this? Laurie shook her head, puzzled. What do you say to a man who is lucky enough to have a nine-year-old daughter? Just that?

"You're lucky. I wish I had a nine-year-old daughter. What happened to her mother?"

He was deathly quiet for a moment, and then he shrugged. "She disappeared five years ago," he said. "I've not seen nor heard from her since."

"Oh, my Lord!" Unconsciously Laurie's hand extended in his direction. His massive flexible hand absorbed it, folding it into his surgeon's paw. He sighed and leaned back in his chair.

"I need someone to help with my daughter," he said. "She's growing up fast. She needs an older woman to guide and direct her."

"Yes, I can understand that," Laurie said. "I was married once myself."

"You have a child too?"

"No."

"And your husband?"

"He—" Laurie bit her lip. There were some things she was not prepared to reveal. "He is no longer—alive."

"Then you're just what I need," he said enthusiastically.

"I think you had better explain that," Laurie said firmly. This little conversation was getting out of hand! She needed more dotted i's and considerably more longer, explanatory sentences.

"Yes. Perhaps I've been too quick," Mason said. He tugged her to her feet and enveloped her in those warm, comfortable arms of his. "I need an adult woman to help take care of my daughter. To act as her mother. To be my hostess." He still had her in his arms.

"Oh? A part-time actress, you mean?"

"Well, I was thinking more of a part-time wife."

"Good heavens!"

"Yes, that too!" He released her and turned back to his desk.

"But I can't—marriage? I hardly know you, and—"

"I was afraid of that," the good doctor said. "Well, perhaps you will change your mind." He nodded politely to her, and went back to his paperwork.

Laurie arrived home late that night, worn out, but not from her studies. Most of her troubles came from actions Dr. Mason had taken on her behalf. Harry, as he'd insisted. Harry. She liked the sound of it, but had no idea why she should ever consider marrying him. Just before she'd left the university, she'd found out what a quick study Harry could be. The academic dean had sent a messenger scurrying after her.

"Dean Williams" the little freshman said. "He wants you in his office."

"Tomorrow," Laurie said. "I'll drop in on him tomorrow."

"Right away," the worried freshman said. "He said *right away quick*!"

"He said—?"

"Right away quick—like, almost at once!"

Easily persuaded, because the academic dean had full control over graduations and credits and unimportant things like that, Laurie headed for the elevator in the administrative tower. By sheer luck the lift was empty.

Sixteen stories higher the machinery disgorged her into the hall just opposite the dean's office. His door was open, and the diminutive old man was standing in it, eyes glued to the elevator shaft. "Well, it's about damn time," the dean said as he ushered her into his outer office. "No calls, Margaret," he added to his secretary as he urged Laurie into his inner sanctum.

Oh, my, Laurie whispered to herself. Something's wrong with my credits. I can't graduate after all!

The dean waved her to a narrow-backed wooden chair, known throughout the student body as the Electric Chair.

"Young lady," the dean said as he riffled through the pile of papers on his desk, "I have been re-examining your records."

"Oh, now what?" Laurie muttered. "They've decided not to accept my transfer credits from the University of Massachusetts!"

"And I've had a long telephone conversation with Dr. Mason." The dean, a tiny beanstalk of a man, tapped the top of his desk with his gold pen.

Sunk, Laurie thought. I wouldn't agree to marry him, and now he's sunk me. Darn that man!

"Dr. Mason is new to the city," the old man went on, "but because of his position he is automatically one of the trustees of this university.'' He cleared his throat, and tapped a time or two more.

Laurie straightened her shoulders and sat up straight in her chair. Go down with the ship, she told herself. Don't let any of them know how much it hurts.

''And he said?'' she prompted.

''And Dr. Mason told me about your performances at the hospital, and the amount of time and effort you have put into this work. Which I have examined. I have computed that you have earned twelve more credits than we had previously recorded.''

A vast sigh escaped from Laurie's lips. ''Twelve more?'' she asked, thinking that the dean might have made a mistake.

''Twelve more,'' the old man agreed. ''Which is six credits more than you need to graduate.'' He began to gather up all the papers on his desk, and shoved them into a file folder.

''And?'' she whispered.

The dean picked up a big rubber stamp, inked it, and slapped it down on the outside of her folder. ''And, Miss Michelson, I do hereby declare that you are a graduate of Grandell University, magna cum laude, as of this moment. Go home and tell your mother.''

''Tell my...?''

The dean smiled, something he did only occasionally, like Leap Year Day. ''Your mother and I,'' he said reflectively, ''were sweethearts in the fifth grade. Now get out of here, Laurie Michelson, and celebrate.''

''Go home and tell your mother!'' Laurie chuckled as she managed to get her old car out of the illegal parking space before the campus police came by with their parking tickets. ''Go home and tell your mother''—what?

That I have graduated. Bachelor of Arts. She had pursued her dream over a period of seven years, through two different universities, and now that she had sailed her ship of state into port she didn't know what to do with it. Who needed a thirty-two-year-old woman with a Bachelor's degree in Performing Arts?

She was so immersed in her problems that she ran a stop sign at Erwin Street and of course a police car was sitting there, waiting just for her. The policeman was a masochist. He pulled away from the curb, juggled his car directly and closely behind her, and then turned on his lights and siren at the same time.

Laurie, still deep in her daydream, almost went through the roof of her car. She jammed on her brakes with enthusiasm, but not with good sense. The officer, too close to react, banged the front of his new Ford patrol car into the massive bumper of her ancient Pontiac. The front end of his practically new car crumpled, and Laurie Michelson arrived home with one Bachelor's degree and three tickets for moving traffic violations.

It was a serious problem, but arguable. The state law stated very plainly that when two cars collided the one in back, which should have maintained a proper distance, was liable. Even if it's a police car? she wondered. And her car had only been moving because he pushed her. Would that sound sensible in court?

After work, three weeks later, Laurie found her mother was not in the living room, as she usually was, with a drink in her hand and a smile on her face. Puzzled, Laurie tracked her down. Maybelle Michelson was sitting at her dressing table in her bedroom, bent over, with tired tears dripping slowly down her cheeks.

"Mother? What is it?"

Her mother straightened up. In one hand she had several envelopes, the glassine type that banks sent out every month. She passed the stack to her daughter.

"I've been a fool," her mother said through the tears.

Laurie patted her gently on the shoulder. "Yes, well, it's been that kind of day for both of us, love. What's this?"

"I just had to have that peach and organdy gown. I just had to, Laurie, darling."

"We all break down once in a while," Laurie responded. "Let me look at this stuff." The top envelope had already been torn open. The insert was one of those little warnings that the banks sent you when you missed a payment. It was dated ten months ago. A mortgage payment. Laurie and her mother had long since agreed that her mother would make the mortgage payments from her father's life insurance, while Laurie would pay for everything else from her odds and ends of income, as best she might.

"So you skipped a payment, love. That's not a criminal offense."

As she spoke gently Laurie was opening the second envelope. It was another warning. "You've missed two payments", Laurie read, and her mother burst out in a freshet of tears.

The third envelope had not been opened. "Mother? You didn't read the rest of these?"

"I thought if I didn't read them the bank would forget," her mother sobbed. "But they didn't!"

"No," Laurie said with a sigh. "With banks it doesn't quite work that way." She reached for the bottom letter. It was stamped with a big "Final Warning", in red. Ten letters. "You haven't paid the mortgage in ten months, Mother?"

"Well, it worked, dear. That one came in two months ago and they haven't sent any more of them since."

A large lump stuck in Laurie's throat. "No, I can see that they wouldn't."

"Well, there were things I just had to have," her mother said defensively. "Dresses and shoes and a new winter coat. I just had to have them, my dear."

"Yes, I can see that, Mother, but if we lose the house…"

Her mother sat up and dashed the tears away. "They

can't do that," she said. "We're a powerful family in this region. I'd die if they took my house. You have to stop them, Laurie. I had always thought you would marry Hans Depner, and he would take care of things." The tears began to flow again, gently but inexorably.

Laurie opened the last envelope and read it carefully. "They've gone to court, Mother, and secured an eviction notice. In two weeks they will auction off the house."

"No!" Mother screamed and fell on the floor. Laurie checked her over, using the flood of information she had picked up at the hospital. Her mother was still breathing. Fainted? Laurie picked her up and helped her over to the bed.

"Lord, do something," Laurie muttered under her breath. "Do something! I can't borrow money from the bank, they're the people who are evicting us. I still owe on my tuition bill at the university. The family car isn't worth selling; my life insurance policy will pay off only 'when death us do part', which seems a hard way to pay off bills. I have no living relatives save Mother. And who in all of great gray Grandell needs a Bachelor of Arts in drama? Who?"

Her mother opened her eyes and moaned, "Laurie? You have to *do* something!"

"Yes, Mother, I'll do something. Go to sleep now. Get some rest." But *what* can I do? she thought. There's nothing to sell, there's no place to borrow. And it might all sound silly, but Mother's position in society is all she lives for. What to do? Marry Hans Depner? Nonsense. He doesn't want to marry me; he wants to get it as a free gift! What to do?

The answer came like an artillery explosion. Who? Dr. Harry Mason!

But…her heart wanted to argue. Cut it out, she demanded of herself. This is desperation time. I'm not a twenty-year-old virgin. Hellfire, I'm not any kind of a virgin. Thirty-two years old; that's really over the hill.

The bloom is already off the roses! I'm probably never going to get another offer!

"Mother, are you awake?"

"Yes."

"I'm going downstairs to make some telephone calls. You stay right here. And don't worry about a thing. I'm sure we can make it all come out right."

Her mother's only answer was a sigh. Laurie tiptoed to the door and shut it behind her. "What a choice," she muttered as she went down the stairs. "Selling yourself so your mother can keep her house? Well, it's better than walking the streets, but— Do Bachelors of Arts get a better price on the street? Funeeee!"

Laurie Michelson scooped the telephone book out from its hiding place under the table. Mason. Harry Mason. It was a brand-new directory and he *was* listed. Her fumble-fingers pushed the right buttons as her mind struggled for the proper words.

Unfortunately Harry Mason didn't answer. Instead a young female picked up the telephone.

"Hello," Laurie said. "I'd like to speak to Dr. Mason, please."

"He don't make house calls," the young voice replied.

"Hey! Don't hang up. I don't have a—a medical problem," Laurie stuttered. "I work at the hospital with—"

"Look, my dad don't have time for no blonde bimbos," the child said. "There's always dozens of nurses and things chasin' after him."

Laurie shook her head. This was obviously not going to be as easy as she had thought, and with the confusion of the day she hardly knew what to say. "I am *not* a blonde bimbo, kid. Your father wanted me to call."

"Yeah, I'll bet he did. Look, lady, my mom and my dad got a divorce, but any day now they're gonna see what a mistake they made, and we'll all be back together. And we don't need no blonde—"

"Redhead," Laurie interrupted.

"But a bimbo just the same," the child said, and the instrument crashed down into its cradle.

Laurie stared at the buzzing instrument in her hand. "Darn," she told herself. "Nothing's easy any more!" She replaced the telephone on its cradle and glared at it. "Why don't I," she asked herself wryly, "have a good cry?"

And so she did.

CHAPTER THREE

THERE is something to be said for perseverance. And perseverance was something Laurie Michelson had in abundance. The day after her battle encounter with Harry Mason's daughter she mustered up her courage, and after displaying to four student groups at the hospital all the aching, coughing symptoms of asthma wandered over into the administrative wing and begged an audience with the chief administrator.

"He's very busy," his secretary said.

Laurie, who had ventured a time or two as a temporary doctor's secretary back in Massachusetts, knew the statement was strictly an opening gambit. After she'd coughed a couple of asthmatic coughs, and reinforced the noise with some grim staring, she gained admission to the holy of holies.

Dr. Harry Mason was sitting back in his swivel chair, his stockinged feet up on his desk, and his shoes in hiding. There was a hole in the heel of his left sock. He was attempting to read his way through a stack of papers, but not doing well at it. His gold-rimmed reading glasses were perched up on his forehead, and his eyes were closed.

"Ahem!" Laurie cleared her throat noisily. One of his eyes opened slowly, and then the other snapped open. His feet came off the desk and his chair straightened up.

"Yes, Miss—?"

Laurie took a deep breath. He had obviously forgotten who she was. And that would never do!

"Michelson," she prompted. "Laurie Michelson."

"Dear Lord, girl, I know *who* you are," he snapped as he came to his feet. "How many other actresses do I have on my payroll?" He slammed the papers down on his desk and glared. "But what, may I ask, do you want?"

"About that subject we—er—were discussing three weeks ago?" she stammered.

He stared at her. "Home help," she prodded.

"Home help? Yes. I have to tell you it's getting worse and worse. I'm being besieged in my own apartment."

"I— Well. You recall we spoke about my university credits, and you were kind enough to call the academic dean…?"

"Something of the sort. I remember vaguely. I make dozens of telephone calls daily."

"Well, he awarded me six credits more than I needed to graduate, but—"

"Good for you," he said, his face sober. And then he just stood there, waiting for her to say something else.

This is not at all what I expected, Laurie told herself. What happened to all the enthusiasm? Her hands were entwined behind her back, tying knots between her fingers. What do I say now?

"The only problem," she said in haste, "is that now I have to pay the graduation fees—"

"Of course," he interrupted, and was quiet again.

"And I don't have a great deal of money," she said at high speed, followed by a deep sigh and a blush. "And you said you required some help at home?"

"I vaguely remember that, and you turned me down."

"I—er—not exactly. I merely—needed time to consider—to talk it over with my mother." An asthmatic cough blocked her brain for a moment. "But now, since I've managed to graduate, I have a great deal more time to invest in—almost anything."

"Ah."

"I'm a very good actress. And—that is, I *will* be graduated if I can pay my tuition bills." Her self-confidence was wearing down at rocket speed. "And now—Lord, the house—"

"What about the house?" His voice was comforting, as if a house couldn't be all *that* much of a problem. Not to him.

So she sniffed a couple of times, knuckled her eyes dry, and told him the whole story. About the house mortgage, and her mother paying for things with her father's life insurance instead of making the mortgage payments, and the bank's foreclosure and the auction, and how—

But of course there was just too much of a problem to be faced, and no sane man would want to put up that much money for a newly graduated actress. Still, she had to ask, and so she did.

"Are you sure you couldn't be satisfied with an actress on a regular basis?"

"I'm not sure of anything at all," he murmured. "My daughter has gone into a flying snit about the whole affair. She doesn't like our apartment, and she misses all the friends she left behind in the army. And she doesn't seem to be all that enthralled with Grandell, for that matter. You were saying?"

"Yes, I thought she might. I—er—talked to her by telephone, and— But marriage is a large and permanent undertaking, and—"

"Indeed it is."

"And I've talked to your daughter, and she's sure that you and your former wife will soon be reconciled—and then you'd have *two* wives, and in this state that's a no-no." She looked up at him expectantly. There was not a single change in his facial expression. "Which is all the more reason—"

"I understand," he said gently but firmly. He walked around his desk and confronted her, nose to nose. Laurie took a faltering step backward.

"My daughter doesn't know everything that goes on in the world. Hellfire, she doesn't even know what goes on in our apartment. There's no chance that my former wife and I will remarry. Or about as much chance as a snowball rolling downhill in hell!"

"Oh?" Laurie squeaked.

"Oh!" he insisted. "I divorced my wife for adultery, and, as far as I know, she's still living with the man in whose bed I found her. I named him as co-respondent in our divorce suit."

"Oh, my," Laurie murmured as she fell back into a chair and grasped both chair-arms with all her strength. "Then you don't think—?"

"No," he said. "Daughters don't know all they think they know. And I think I might be interested in a proposition—if you're a good enough actress—to impersonate a wife for, say, four or five years? Interested?"

"I— That's a long time," Laurie returned.

He shrugged his broad shoulders. "There has to be some considerable time invested," he said. "My daughter is just approaching that age when she needs some stability in our home. Puberty, you know."

"I know."

"Ideally, then, perhaps a marriage of convenience," he suggested. "Until the child is perhaps more mature?"

"That's a thought," she said, and for the first time he smiled. It made all the difference in the world, as if during a thunderstorm the sun had broken through Culver Gap, and scattered warmth throughout the valley. But his smile faded quickly.

"It's a thought," he said, "but not much of one. I could see some temporary approach, say until my daughter is either twenty-one or she marries?"

"But that's—she's nine years old now? You're talking twelve years minimum! That's a long time to maintain a cover!"

"What cover?"

"Well—you know—a marriage of convenience!"

"I don't plan to make it all *that* convenient," he said. "My daughter is a clever little girl. The only thing that will convince her is the real thing, or something so close to it that even we can't tell the difference."

Laurie folded her hands together and settled back in the chair. I need the money, she told herself desperately. My mother needs the money. I don't have enough to buy myself a winter coat. It doesn't get to be as cold here in Tennessee as it does in New England, but it *does* get cold. And Mother—all she has left is the grace of living in her old-fashioned style! There's a mortgage on the house, and I can't pay either it or the gas bill or—

In two weeks we'll lose the house! The only thing I own outright is a ten-year-old car. What am I going to tell Mother? That her only child can't support her?

She moistened her lips. "So a temporary marriage is all you're willing to offer?"

"Not all," he said quietly. "There's a lot of compensation. Full financial support for you and your mother. Companionship. Maintenance of your mother's social position."

"But that's for my mother. What about me?"

"There could be the joy of the rest of the children." He leaned back against the desk and smiled again. Laurie felt the blush crowd up into her brain. God, why was he grinning like a crocodile? And then her brain caught up.

"The rest of the children?" she sputtered.

"The rest of the children."

"But—you mean— This marriage. Sex and everything?"

"As you say. Sex and everything. You can't see that?"

"But I don't even love you!"

"I never knew that to be a block against having sex and children. In fact, I never did find love to be anything but extra baggage. Half the United States was settled on arranged marriages in the early days. Any mom would do.''

Two tears formed, one in each of Laurie's eyes. He traced them with his surgeon's eye as they drifted down to her cheeks and jumped off into space. She knew he was right; any mom would do, from his and his daughter's standpoint. But she resented his being so right!

But I need the money, she told herself. Need it quickly. And the only alternative to this so-called marriage is— And she didn't want to think about the alternative. Wearily she shrugged. There was no choice at all. And he is, she told herself, trying to look on the bright side, a well-set man. And steadily employed! She sniffed away her tears and settled back in the chair.

''I have a very large number of debts,'' she said softly.

''It doesn't matter. I'd be glad to help pay them.''

Laurie took a deep breath. *Help* pay them? That would hardly meet her needs, would it?

''I—don't think I can jump in head first like that. How about a trial period—say, a ninety-day trial?'' There was the sound of rage quivering in her voice. His eyes sparked at her as if he recognized the rage. He has no right to be forcing me, she thought. No right! But—?

''On my terms?''

''On your terms,'' she agreed.

''And if the ninety-day trial works?''

''To the satisfaction of the three of us, then I will be willing to renew the arrangement for a—four-year period.''

''Fair enough. And if you feel that you want a renewal option at the end of that time I think I could consider it.''

''Don't do me any favors,'' Laurie Michelson said harshly as she glared at him from across the desk.

''Perhaps a kiss to seal the bargain?'' he offered.

"No, thanks," Laurie muttered. "I'd sooner kiss a rattlesnake. What I'd rather see is a signed contract."

"You don't sound too jolly, Laurie. I'm not going to force you into this, you know."

"No. I can always refuse, can't I? And find myself out on the street."

"But you said you'd been married once before. I can't believe that all this is such a terrifying experience."

"My last experience of marriage was a total catastrophe," she told him. "Total." Her voice cracked, and she coughed again.

"You don't care to tell me about it?"

"No, I certainly do not!"

"But you are still willing to give it all a try?"

She gave a hesitant and soft "Yes".

"Then all we need to do is sign the contract and find a house to—"

"House!" She gulped. "I forgot that."

"Well, you shouldn't. I'm living downtown in a disgusting little apartment, which is another thing that my daughter hates. Now if, as you say, your family house is up for auction, suppose I buy it and we all move in together? Big house, is it?"

"Enormous. Six bedrooms, two sitting rooms, two acres of land, an Olympic-size swimming pool, two baths. Built just before the Civil War, and augmented half a dozen times, and—"

"Just the thing," he interrupted. "Just the thing."

"The auction is in two weeks," she said hesitantly. "On the house, I mean. Do you think—?"

"No problem." He thumbed through the little desk calendar. "I think perhaps in a couple of days we could begin this little ninety-day trial."

"A couple of days?" she gasped.

"Day after tomorrow," he agreed. "I have a large number of operations scheduled in the next three or four weeks."

"And we mustn't upset the patients," she said numbly.

"Exactly."

"I— Whenever," she agreed softly as she shrugged in despair.

"Then I'll scribble out the ninety-day contract, including the option to renew, and Mary Beth can type it out for us. No big ceremony, unless it all works out well—maybe something small, in the hospital chapel?"

"I don't care, but—how am I going to tell my mother?"

He peered at his wristwatch. "I have a couple of hours, Laurie. Why don't you come along with me now and I'll tell her?"

It wasn't really a question. He took her arm, pulled her out of the chair, and hustled her out of the office.

"Dr. Mason," his secretary called after him as he stepped out into the corridor.

"Later, Mary Beth," he returned. "I have to see about an engagement."

There were several hospital employees in the corridor who heard the entire statement. A subtle buzz followed them all the way to the outer door.

Mrs. Michelson— "Call me Maybelle," she had insisted just after the doctor's third sentence—fluttered around him like an over-age butterfly. "Engagement?" she repeated. "Oh, Laurie! How wonderful! And when is the wedding—?"

"We haven't quite come to that," Laurie hastened to say. "There are a number of things to be straightened out, and we have to convince—" And she stopped there. It was an embarrassment to admit she didn't know the child's name.

"Suzanne," he inserted. "We call her Sukie."

"Yes, the doctor has a nine-year-old daughter. Sukie, she's called. And she—doesn't care a bean for me?"

"Doesn't know about it as yet," he said. "So we have

to tell her the happy news, and get her settled down. In fact, Mrs. Michelson, we're all cramped up in a little downtown apartment, and Laurie and I thought when your house comes up for auction we might buy it, and set ourselves up as one happy family!''

"How wonderful," Maybelle gushed. "It isn't often that a newly married couple want to have their mother-in-law living with them!''

"Yes, well, beggars can't be choosers," he said, with a chuckle.

But the word "beggars," which had once meant nothing at all to Maybelle Michelson, had, in the last few weeks, become an open wound. "Beggars? But surely a doctor, and a hospital administrator, and— Beggars?''

He waved a casual hand. "Metaphorically speaking," he commented. "I—we—have more than enough money to get along with. Bonuses, military retirement pay, hospital salary, and of course I'll be doing some outside consulting work, you know."

Maybelle, who had been holding her breath since *that* word appeared, began to breathe again. Her laugh was still pitched high and brassy. "Then let me offer you some wine, Doctor. My—er—Laurie's father put it down some twenty years ago and—''

But by that time Laurie had circled behind her mother's chair, waved her hands, made choking motions at her throat and negative gestures with her hair flying.

"No, I don't think so," the good doctor reported. "I still have work to do at the hospital, and alcohol is not approved of, eh?''

"Lucky," Laurie said as he escorted her out to his car. "My father was a wonderful man, but I think he made that wine from powders in his chemistry set. Wave your hand. Mother is standing behind the curtains at the window."

Harry Mason was grinning as he helped her into the passenger seat of his car. "Never gives up, does she?''

"Never. She's been trying to get me married again for, oh, the past two years. Persistent, my mother."

"But not you?"

"Me? I wouldn't know the meaning of the word!"

"Thank God for that. Two persistent people in one house is enough; Sukie is what I would call super-persistent." He swung the wheel of his Cadillac and headed down Erwin Street, going toward downtown.

"Watch this corner," she advised. "There's a—"

And there he was, standing beside his banged-up prowl car, as disgruntled a policeman as one could ever hope to see. So Laurie turned in her seat and waved to him gaily. He took his hat off and wiped its rim with a handkerchief before waving back.

"Friend of yours?" Harry asked as he cut across Pleasant Street and drove into the parking lot of the Montmorency apartment building, the biggest housing unit in the city, and the newest—if you could call forty years old new.

"A nodding acquaintance," she replied. "My. A big place, isn't it?"

"Has to be," he returned as he leaned across her and opened her door. "Has to be to support the rentals." His grin seemed to signal a joke; it failed. In the leaning and opening he had managed to brush his arm delicately across her breasts, and Laurie's ears had disconnected as everything north of her shoelaces came to attention. *He* didn't seem bothered at all, but men, she knew, were funny that way.

He came around to her side of the car, took her elbow in his strong surgeon's grip and led her toward the front of the building. "All kinds of little shops on the ground floor," he announced. "Something I have to buy for you before we go upstairs."

"Could we perhaps go a little slower?" she gasped. "My legs are a little shorter than yours and I can't keep up."

"Oh. Window-shopping?" He pulled her to a stop at the first window. "Like that one? Now there's something I'd like to see you in."

Laurie gulped. The model figure displayed a half-bikini—the bottom half, of course. For a girl her size Laurie displayed what her first husband had called a well-rigged top. He'd said it so much that every thought in that direction still left her embarrassed. As now.

"Hey, you don't like that? How about this dress?"

"This dress" was a tasty little black thing with no back and no real front—at least until it reached the navel, but from that point it swept down to the ankles with enthusiasm.

"No? Going to be hard to please, are you?"

"I'm afraid so," she agreed. "It gets cold in this part of Tennessee, and I sincerely believe if we *were* married you wouldn't want me to walk around with such little covering. I'm—a big girl, in case you hadn't noticed."

"Oh, I noticed," he said, and those deep-set eyes of his gleamed like a hunting lion's. "On the very first day we met, I noticed." He put her in motion again by towing her. "But maybe something like that for the bedroom?" She started to answer but he held up his free hand. "No, not in the bedroom either. I'd prefer that we wear nothing at all in the bedroom."

"Well, really!" She pulled her hand free and marched along with both hands clenched into fists.

"I said something wrong?"

She chose her words carefully. "No, perhaps not wrong, but certainly premature, wouldn't you think?"

"Ah. Rushing, am I? Well, this is the place I wanted you to see."

A jewelry store. An expensive jewelry store. The display window featured only a single diamond necklace resting on a black platform. Even the doorknobs said, "I cost a lot." Unless the diamonds were glass? She didn't dare to ask.

The floor manager knew him well. "Harry," he said as he came forward with hand outstretched. "Is this the time?"

"This is the time, Benny. Do you have it?"

"This way." He led them into the back of the store, stopping for a minute at the edge of the brilliantly lighted area to appraise Laurie from foot to feathers. "Yeah," he said enthusiastically. "How about this?"

He reached into the back case and took out a tiny square box. "There."

"Open it," Harry directed. "It cost two appendix removals and one heart angioplasty."

"Me?" Laurie stepped back from the counter a pace or two.

"Of course you," Harry insisted. "There are darn few men who wear this sort of thing."

"We searched the whole of the USA to locate that," Benny interjected. "But Harry always was particular."

Warily Laurie picked up the box. "The whole of the USA?" They both nodded. She tried to flip up the cover and managed to break a fingernail, but when her struggle was concluded a single pearl set in a platinum ring stared at her. "Is this where I say, For *me?*" she gasped.

"That's what you say," Harry said. "Lord, are you slow." He reached over her shoulder and plucked the ring out. And then hesitated. "I forget what finger this goes on," he apologized. Laurie, somewhat in a daze, offered him her left hand.

"The—the last time anybody o-offered me a ring like this," she stammered as he slipped it on her finger, "it came in a cracker box."

"It's real," the salesman assured her. "A natural pearl set in platinum, with diamond chips."

"You mean that *he* didn't get you a ring?" Harry asked.

"Only a gold ring for the ceremony," she said, sighing. "He said it belonged to his mother. Turned out to be *a* mother's ring all right, but not *his* mother's. They took it away when they came for him.''

"They?''

"I don't care to talk about that,'' Laurie said as her brain meshed with her tongue and put an end to the conversation.

"Of course not,'' Harry said. "Well, thank you, Benny. Now we have to go upstairs and explain it all to Madame DeFarge.''

"Madame who?''

"You don't read much fiction about the French Revolution? Madame sat under the guillotine and knitted— Forget it. We're going to take this up and display it to my daughter, and see if she might possibly agree to our marriage. It's a smaller ring than her mother's. She'll like that. Perhaps you won't?''

"If you have to bring it back, will you lose a lot of money?'' Laurie asked anxiously.

"Dear Lord,'' Harry muttered as he snatched up her right hand and towed her back onto the sidewalk.

"Well, I don't want you to go bankrupt over an unimportant little fake wedding,'' she said firmly.

"I swear I won't and it's not unimportant and I don't think it will be a fake wedding,'' he retorted as he propelled her into the lobby of the building and up to the bank of elevators, two of which seemed to be working.

"But before we go up,'' he said as he pulled her close, close enough to weld them together, close enough to flatten her ample breasts against the solid steel of his chest, "I need this for luck.'' And he kissed her. It lasted for hours. Well, perhaps minutes, she told herself later. But it seemed like hours at the time. And there was more than simple affection involved in the whole affair. Her knees were still shaking as the elevator in front of them hissed to a stop and opened its door.

He carried her across the threshold. "Everybody's watching,'' she whispered in his ear.

"Everybody who?" he asked. Her feet were three or four inches above the floor, putting her mouth just at his ear. It seemed that he might never put her down. "Who?" he repeated.

"Everybody in the corridor, and everybody in—"

"Hush," he said. "There's nobody in the elevator but us, and I didn't see anyone in the corridor. Hold still. I can't do this when you're wiggling." So she did and he did, and the elevator bell rang at the fifth floor, where a group of people got in and applauded as the door closed and the machine started back toward the first floor.

"Were we supposed to get off?" she asked, red-faced, her nose about two inches from his and her feet still miles from the floor.

"Sooner or later," he commented. So they rode down to the ground floor, where he kissed her again, and then back to the fifth again. "Good luck," the little crowd they had delivered down called. And this time when they reached the fifth floor he stuck his foot in the door mechanism and they stared at each other wordlessly until she had recovered her breath.

"Typical hospital procedure," she panted.

"Typical?"

"I've been in a number of hospitals," she explained. "Each time my doctor, for whom I was paying a lot of money, introduced me to the expensive surgeon, and then *he* introduced me to the expensive anesthesiologist, and then to the three expensive nurses, and having hired all that expensive help they wheeled me over to the operating room and everybody said, 'Good luck!' With all those experts and all that money I needed 'Good Luck' as well?"

"You're making that up. Turn right and down the hall. Please."

"Please? All of a sudden please? What happened to the dictator?"

His face flushed blood-red. "I am not," he said

firmly, "a dictator. Doctors are not dictators. Some of them aren't, anyway." And then, after another kiss, he said, "There's nothing worse than a lip-flapper. Hush. Do you have the ring on? Push the buzzer button."

"I am not a gabble-monger. If you would put me down, you could push the button for yourself. Yes, I'm wearing the ring. Do I flash it around so it can be readily seen?" He let her slip down the length of him until she was standing free. "You did that on purpose," she snapped.

"Did what?"

"Let me slide down you as if you were a fireman's pole."

"Yeah. Sexy, wasn't it?"

It was, really, but rather than let him know it she industriously struggled to rearrange her clothes. Her mind, usually world-class, fumbled for a rebuttal without success. Something about "I don't deal in sexism", but it wouldn't come out just the way she wanted it. "And I—" she started to say, but the door swung open.

"Well," the strident little voice said. "Here's my dad with another blonde bimbo!" The girl herself was not all that little. Five feet, more or less, with blonde hair falling down to her waist in fluffy curls, a pair of red denims just a bit too short for her, and a chunky figure that might eventually expand in all the right directions—if she lived that long.

Laurie waited for a moment to let Harry Mason get in the first words. Instead he stood quietly behind her. Laurie glared at him; he glared back.

"Well? Do you intend to say something, blondie, or shall I shut the door?"

"Redhead," Laurie said. "Shut up, kid!" She elbowed her way through the door. The girl retreated in front of her. The girl's father, with a large smirk on his face, followed behind and dived for a chair.

"Go ahead, you two," he invited. "Nothing I like better than a good squabble."

"Red-headed bimbo," Sukie mused. "Did I talk to you recently on the telephone?"

"The very one," Laurie acknowledged. "Did you have lunch?"

"Peanut butter sandwich," the child said. "Not even any jelly on. What kind of a pig-pen are we living in?"

"A lot like Fort Smith before they closed it," her father reminisced. "What happened to the woman I hired yesterday to look after you?"

"She quit. Couldn't stand the traffic. No guts."

"That's no way to talk," he said, and then turned to Laurie. "See what I mean? She has all the manners of an army mule."

"Don't talk like that," Laurie muttered at him. "She's only a child—"

"My Lord, Pop," the child interrupted. "You really screwed up with this one. She talks back. What are you going to do now, lady?"

"Well, among other things," Laurie said, "I'm going to marry your father, and I'm going to take you both over to my house and out of this cardboard box you're living in. Go get yourself a nightgown and a toothbrush. We can send somebody else over tomorrow to pack up for you. Oh, and a jacket and clean jeans. It's starting to turn cool now that we are getting towards the end of September— Git."

"'Git'? What kind of talk is that? Daddy?"

"Git," Harry Mason said.

The child hesitated, leaning back and forth as if unable to make up her mind.

"And stop in the bathroom," Laurie added.

"Daddy!" the child screamed as she fled down the corridor.

"Well, now," Harry Mason said. "I hadn't expected

that.'' He got up lazily from the couch and came over to Laurie. "But it seemed to work.''

"For the moment,'' she responded, edging cautiously away from him.

His arms were longer than her sidestepping feet. He caught and kissed her again, just as Sukie came back into the room stuffing a nightgown into a backpack.

"Hey, this is seriouser than I thought," the child said. "What have you did now, Dad?"

"Done, not did," he said, sighing. "The world changes every day."

"B-but..." Sukie stammered as Laurie flashed her new ring in front of the child's huge eyes. "Hah! My mom had a bigger ring than that."

"I'm sure she did," Laurie said softly. "And deserved it. You must have loved her a very great deal."

"Better 'n you."

"I don't doubt it, Sukie. I'll try to make things better."

"Come on, let's go," Harry said. "It's getting late and I still have a couple of consultations."

Harry took Laurie's hand and started for the door. Sukie, still trailing her backpack, followed along, a puzzled look squirreling around on her chunky face.

CHAPTER FOUR

MAYBELLE MICHELSON was sitting in the downstairs lounge, coiled up around a double martini, when Laurie, Harry Mason and the child came into the house.

"Well, what have we here?" she said as she lurched unsteadily to her feet.

"Big house," Sukie Mason commented. "Stretches, like, for ever, don't it?"

"What a lovely boy," Maybelle said, toasting the child with her martini glass.

"Boy, are we in big trouble," Sukie snarled. "A lush for a grandmother? As it happens, lady, I ain't a boy. I'm a girl. Anybody can see that."

"I don't see how anybody can see that." Maybelle giggled. "You wear ragged jeans like most boys. You have long hair like most boys. You have dirt on your nose like most boys. Obviously you're a boy." She emptied her glass. "And, Doctor, there's a call from your office. Some sort of accident." With which the lady of the manor set her empty glass down firmly on the table and swished out of the room.

"Wow," Sukie said.

"Where's the telephone?" Dr. Mason asked.

"Behind the couch on the floor," Laurie answered. "Come on, Sukie, let me show you your room."

"Three-car accident," the good doctor reported as he set the phone down again. "Six people. I've got to get back to the emergency room."

"Well, just like old times," Sukie commented as the

front door closed behind him. "You got a cook in this palace?"

"Yeah. Me." Laurie sighed. "You hungry?" Sukie nodded. "Then follow me."

The kitchen was at the back of the house, refurbished in the 1950s, and again in the 1990s, just before Laurie's father died. It was now equipped with natural gas cooking stoves, floor heaters, and a wall covered by shining copper-bottomed pans. The pans glistened, but none of the gas appliances worked. "Because we haven't paid the gas bills," Laurie explained drily.

"Your mother keeps all this stuff shining?"

"Well, not exactly," Laurie said apologetically. "We had a housekeeper."

"Oh? But she's not here?"

"No. She only comes when we can pay her. And this is not her week."

"So how are you going to make me somethin' to eat?"

"Over there," Laurie pointed. "We have that little electric cooker, and we *have* paid the electric bill. How about a plate of ham and eggs?"

"Tell me," the girl said suspiciously. "Ham 'n' eggs? That's big-time eating. How do you afford that?"

"You don't understand, Sukie. We live on the very edge of town and we run a sort of farm. We have chickens. They lay eggs. We have several pigs. We slaughtered one about a month ago, and that's where we get our ham. We have a vegetable garden out back. Delia's husband Buddy does the outside work for us. He takes some of the products instead of pay."

"But good Lord, that means a heck of a lot of work!"

"Oh, a middlin' amount. We make our own bread, for example. It would be cheaper to buy bread at the market, but my mother loves fresh home-made bread. So we bake our own."

"Me too," the girl replied. "I'd love to have a plate of ham 'n' eggs and toast, and—whatever."

"And whatever," Laurie echoed, laughing as she reached for her apron, and one for Sukie. The ham was easy, but the little girl had never struggled with real eggs. Laurie gave a lesson, and within minutes the table was set...and in another five minutes was cleaned off.

"Now that's some livin'," the little girl said, puffing out her cheeks and stomach to emphasize her enjoyment. "Country style, that's the way. Now what?"

"Now we wash the dishes, kiddo."

"Wash the...? I ain't never done that. I don't know if my dad would want me to do that." There was a brief pause while she mustered more excuses. "My mother never washed no dishes either."

"Peculiar mother," Laurie said as she got up and walked over to the sink.

"Hey, don't you say nothin' about my mother!"

"Then don't you say anything about my mother either," came the riposte. "Fair's fair."

"Well, I don't know about that. We didn't have no dishes at the apartment. We had paper plates and paper cups and stuff like that."

"We do occasionally use paper plates," Laurie admitted. "Especially when we have a picnic out in the backyard. But that's not today. Today we wash dishes—and we have to hurry because we have to make up a room for you and your dad."

"Oh, boy," the child half protested. "I didn't plan to hire out like no day-laborer."

"That's the way the cookie crumbles," Laurie teased, and led the way to the kitchen sink. The work, which began with a grumble, ended up with song and laughter. The kitchen was almost immaculate when Laurie noticed the clock. "Oh, my," she muttered as she stripped off her apron and started for the door.

"Now what?" Sukie asked.

"I have a class at the hospital this afternoon."

"So skip it for once. The teacher will never know."

"I'm the teacher."

"Well, that's a fine kettle of fish!"

"It is, isn't it? Come along and I'll show you your room. You can be doing the sheets and pillows while I'm at the hospital, right?"

"Yeah, sure." The retort was not exactly cheerful, but, having been shown the room, the hall linen closet, and the towels for the bathroom, Sukie began, at exaggerated slow speed, to do something about it. Laurie shook her head, checked her watch, and went off on her way, with both sets of fingers crossed.

The first person she met, standing out on the verandah, was Dr. Mason.

"Hi," he called out. Not a cheerful greeting, but something's better than nothing, she told herself.

"Things settled down in Emergency?"

"Yeah. We lost three of them. High-school kids having a joyride on a bottle of vodka and a twenty-year-old car. One of them was barely fourteen." He bowed his head and blinked his eyes for a moment. He looked up and found it hard to speak. "How's Sukie coming along?"

She was about to tell him all about it, when she noticed that weary look in his eyes. He *is* sensitive, she told herself. He's still all wrapped up with those kids. And then he opened his arms and she went into them, bringing along the fullness of her compassion and the warmth of her lips.

"God," he said a few minutes later, "I needed that."

"Me too," she admitted. "Oh, my, look at the time! I'm late! I'm late!"

He grinned as he patted her gently on her fundament to speed her on her way. "You don't look like a rabbit," he called after her. "See you at supper?"

That phrase followed her all through her rush to outfit

herself for her diagnostic class. "I'm late! I'm late!"
"You don't look like a rabbit." And while the student
doctors were playing tag with the symptoms of rubella
which she was tastefully displaying out of her make-up
kit and a broken thermometer she herself was running
through her list of quotations until she finally came
ashore on *Alice's Adventures in Wonderland* and the
white rabbit.

All of which brought her home at seven o'clock, to
face a flustered family of faces, all screaming, "What's
for dinner?" And Laurie had no idea in the world, for
the subject had never come up in so crowded a fashion
in all her many years of making do in the kitchen.
"Welsh rarebit?" she suggested. A chorus of groans returned, but Laurie ignored them and got to work.

"I don't want to eat no bunny rabbit," Sukie complained.

"It isn't rabbit," her father said. "It's a sort of cheese
dish. You'll like it."

"You always say that."

"Say what?"

"Oh, you always say, 'you'll like it.' I never tasted
none of it, so how can you say I'll like it?"

"Sukie, you'll eat it. You'll like it!" It was a command from on high, from a tired father who had no intention of pampering a little girl.

"Will I really like it, Laurie?"

"I think so, love. Try it. If you don't like it we'll find
something else. Bargain?"

"Yeah, bargain." The child rolled up her sleeve, spat
in the palm of her hand, and offered the hand to Laurie.
You don't catch me with old-fashioned tricks, Laurie
told herself as she repeated the move and clasped the
little hand.

"Ugh," Maybelle Michelson said, shrinking away
from the table.

"It's an old-fashioned down-country way of sealing a bargain, Mother."

"I understand that," Maybelle retorted. "But at the dinner table?"

"Mother!"

An uneasy silence ruled the table for ten minutes or more, until the doctor broke the ice. "And did everyone get settled in a room?" he asked.

"All but you," his daughter piped up. "And Laurie, she has the biggest bed I ever saw in my whole life. Yours is almost as big."

Dr. Mason shook his head in disgust. "Put my foot in it the first time around," he murmured just loud enough for Laurie to hear. "What do I say next?"

"Try whistling three verses of Dixie," Laurie said sarcastically, "and then come right out with the whole truth. Or as little of the truth as you think you can get away with!"

"Some mystery?" Sukie, seeing the embarrassment on the faces of the adults, pushed for all she was worth. "Tell me, Laurie. Tell me the mystery!"

"No mystery," Laurie said as she served each of them a plate of Welsh rarebit. "Your dad and I are engaged to be married, so we're going to share a room when we get married. His room is for privacy and my closet isn't big enough to hold Harry's clothes and mine."

A considerable amount of adult breath-holding followed as they all stared at the little girl, expecting an explosion. She looked them all in the eye, one after the other, and said, "Oh," as she reached for her knife and fork and dug in.

The adults at the table seemed frozen in position. "Eat, eat," Sukie commanded. "It's good."

Cutlery clattered, and a conversational buzz arose.

Until another roadblock brought everything to a standstill. "You gonna marry my dad?"

"Believe I will."

"My mother won't like that."

"Do you say so?"

"Do I hafta call you Mama?"

"Not if you don't want to. It's entirely up to you, Sukie. If you can't go for Mama, or Mom, how about just plain Laurie?"

"Look, I've got to fill out my notes on these last three cases," the doctor said. "You'll excuse me?" And before anyone could vote a single yea or nay he pushed back his chair and was gone.

"My mother said she saw less of him than the butler," Sukie said, sighing.

"I believe it," Laurie said with a sigh. "Seems to be the way of life for doctors. Emergencies arise and surgery is needed. And with only two surgeons it's impossible to leave a patient who's in pain or dying. This can happen at night, early morning and holidays too. They can't take much time out for families and vacations. Would you want him to leave someone in pain or dying?"

Sukie shook her head reluctantly. "I don't think so."

Maybelle retired early. The addition of one little girl had worn her to a frazzle. Laurie helped her up the stairs.

"Maybe we could send her to a boarding school," Mrs. Michelson suggested. It was a trial balloon, Laurie could tell. Something to float in the air, to see who agreed and who disagreed. On this particular occasion it fell rather flat. "Or send her off to the YWCA camp?"

"I don't think so, Mother."

"Well, how about if we send her off to her mother?"

"That's not an option. Face up to it, Ma, she's ours for years and years. It's the price for keeping the house and getting the roof fixed. Go to bed, love. By tomorrow it'll seem different."

"Yes. Worse. And Laurie, it's true that you're going to share a room with him?"

"All true."

"But what am I going to tell the ladies in the women's club?"

"Mention the magic word: *marriage.*"

"Ah." And as Maybelle went off to her room Laurie could see that the mind of the Michelson mother was already hard at work, embroidering a solution for the strange menagerie now suddenly accumulated under her roof.

Within three days the new mixture of people in the Michelson house had rattled and rotated and rolled, and the dominant personality, Sukie, had risen to the top. She had also found three soulmates—the Harrington boys, who lived at the bottom of the hill.

"My mother feels," Laurie said tentatively on the first evening that she managed to trap the doctor in the house, "that your daughter is associating with a bad crowd. Mainly the Harrington boys. Do you have any thoughts on the matter?"

He put down his papers, looked at her over his half-glasses, and said, "No."

"You don't mind?"

"I said no, meaning I don't have any ideas. Children mix and rub off their sharp edges on each other all the time. Despite what your mother thinks we have no royal families in the United States. That's God's design."

"Oh, really? I didn't realize you were in such close communion with the Deity."

He looked down his patrician nose at her. "The children are your responsibility, Laurie."

"Oh? Even though there's only one, and it happens to be yours?"

"Even though. Go away. I've got a million papers to write, and five thousand government forms to fill out."

"Do you suppose you might consider this?" She

slipped a bill under the bottom of the pile with which he was dealing.

"What?"

"Gas bill. We heat and cook with natural gas. It's getting cold around these parts."

"How much is it?"

"A whole lot."

"Speaking of which, the day after tomorrow they auction off the house—a little earlier than planned. Anything to say before I go off to challenge the bank dragons?"

"Don't bid too much. The roof leaks in four places."

"That's it?"

"That's enough."

"I suppose it is. And, speaking of payments, it's time you made one."

"I don't understand."

"You do, but you just hope it'll go away. It won't. Pucker up."

So she did and he did and it was altogether exciting for a woman who had missed a great deal of that sort of thing in the past few years. And it was plain to see, at least to Laurie, that Dr. Mason was a past master of the sport.

"And tonight," he added, "when it's deep-breathing time, I'll be joining you in our bed."

Laurie gulped. *"Our bed?"* Something was blocking her esophagus, no doubt, and there was a medical man right there at hand, but she had no intention of asking for a consultation. Instead she ran upstairs at flank speed, and fumbled through all the things she hadn't used since her husband died. After all, she told herself, with all the complex contracts in force hereabouts, there was surely no reason to risk pregnancy at this early date. And so a shower and then to bed.

The old grandfather clock in the hall sounded a solid eleven o'clock when she managed to put her head down on her pillow. She tossed and turned. Outside the window a storm had risen to haunt her. It banged at the loose windows in their frames, and rattled threats for an hour. And just before she managed to fall asleep another thought struck her. After all, it had been a lot of years since her last husband, and she had no idea what the good doctor preferred.

So she climbed back out of bed, did her hair up in a tight knot to keep him from rolling over on it, debated her transparent chinois nightgown, and traded it off for a heavy flannel nightshirt. No, it wasn't really that cold just at the moment, but a girl had to take no chances.

When the clock struck one she was still fussing. Sleep was eluding her like two coal trains passing on opposite tracks. But still he didn't come.

Finally the big clock struck two in the morning. Laurie Michelson blinked one eye too many and fell asleep. And *then* he came, a quiet ghost accustomed to stealing through the wards without awakening patients. He stood beside the bed and watched her toss and turn, then went over to the bureau to finger the various boxes she had put to use. As he stripped off his clothing and let it fall where it might, he dictated a little note to himself on his pocket recorder.

"Remind Laurie," he half whispered, "that latex products over two years old lose their tensile strength and have to be replaced."

At which point, stark naked, he climbed into the bed with a shark's grin on his face, but before the shark could bite he too promptly fell asleep. There was a lot of that going around on Jackson Street, or so it seemed, and there were bound to be troubles to follow.

Laurie came up out of her dreams not more than an hour after sunrise. Harry had gone, if he had ever been there. The pillows were roughed up on the other side of the bed—her only evidence. And if he had done *that* while she slept she had no way of knowing. So she sat up in the soft wide bed and stretched, and Sukie appeared, clutching her worn and torn teddy bear by the left foot. The child was dressed in a half-buttoned red and white pajama set which had seen too much wear and tear.

"You slept with my daddy," she accused.

"Well, we had to sleep somewhere, love."

"You got plenty of empty bedrooms in this house and his is next door. Plenty."

"But not plenty of mattresses and sheets and blankets, Sukie. It's chilly this morning. Climb up here with me, why don't you?"

The child threw her bear on ahead of her and then climbed up for herself. After much squirming the pair of them settled down next to each other. The child was a full-blown oven, set at high heat. Laurie moved away for comfort, and hoped. But Sukie had no intention toward peace and goodwill. She attacked immediately.

"You know what?"

"No, what?" Laurie asked.

"When my real mommy and dad slept in the same bed they used to wake up in the morning together, and then they would have a wrestling match."

"Wrestling match? Well, now, I'm a late sleeper. It sort of rules out early-morning wrestling."

"Well, Daddy loved it. He almost always won. And then he'd be up and about, all cheery and whistling, and go off to work."

"I can picture that. And Mommy enjoyed it too?"

"Naw. She made believe like she did, and smiled and stuff until after he had gone, and then she would say some nasty words and duck down under the blankets and not get up until noontime."

Quiet settled across the house. Mrs. Michelson hardly ever got out of bed before noon, but Laurie wanted her cup of coffee, and hated the economy that had cut out the maid who'd formerly fetched it.

"Now why is it, Sukie, that you're telling me all this?"

"You ain't the first blonde bimbo my dad set up to play house with. I'm sorta tired of them—change after change. You know. A week or two of 'Let's be friends, Sukie', and then whomp, and there's a new face. I hardly could remember what their names were. So I thought that if you and I had a real man-to-man talk every now and then you could avoid some of the errors, and—who knows?—you might last a month or so. You got a lot of potential."

"Red-headed bimbo," Laurie coaxed absent-mindedly. "Man-to-man?"

"Yeah."

"Give me a 'for instance'."

"I just did. Dad likes to wrestle in the morning."

"I see. And tomorrow you'll give me another tip?"

"If you last that long," the girl said morosely. "I can't see you havin' a lot of luck. Dad really likes blondes. You could dye your hair maybe?"

"I'd hate to do that," Laurie said sadly. "I'm pretty attached to my red hair. No pun intended, you understand." She threw off the blankets. "Well, let's scoot down to the kitchen and see what we can see."

"So why not?" The pair of them padded down the stairs together, friends for ever—at least for the moment. And received another surprise. Tied to one leg of the kitchen table by a dirty ball of string was a mongrel dog. The dog was dirtier than the string, and scratched a great deal.

"Now where did *he* come from?" Sukie asked with that innocent tone of voice that children used when they obviously knew just *where* the animal had come from.

"Fleas," Laurie commented. "No collar. No license. He needs to be de-loused, fumigated, shot—"

"Oh, not that," Sukie cried. "He's a nice fella. You can't just shoot him 'cos you don't like dogs!"

"Oh, I like dogs very much," Laurie mused. "Very much. And the kind of shooting I was talking about was inoculation shots. It's a legal requirement. Where did you find him?"

"On the street corner. A big car came around the corner and somebody inside opened the door and throwed him out. Wasn't that a awful thing to do?"

"Awful," Laurie agreed. "People like that ought to be horse-whipped!"

"Do you think—my dad…?"

"Would allow you to keep him?"

"Yeah. Of course, it's your house, and if you say yes I'm sure my dad—"

"Ah, little darling, you still don't have it right. It's your father's house—or it will be in a day or so. And you're your father's daughter, so Dad has the last approval."

"Ugh!"

"Yes, there's that too." There was a moment of thought. "Your dad was an army man, right?"

"Right."

"Well, when I was in university up in Massachusetts I joined the Reserve Officers Training Corps."

"Why would you do a stupid thing like that?"

"Because I needed three easy credits. That's the story of my life, seems to me. Three easy credits. Well, anyway, the one thing I noticed was that army officers in charge of the training didn't know a great deal about the equipment we had. But they *did* know if it was bright and shiny."

"So we have to polish and shine Armand?"

"Armand? What kind of a name is that?"

"Well, he's gotta have a name, right? And he has that sort of French look, so I named him Armand."

"OK by me, love, but Armand is a boy's name, and this dog of yours is definitely a girl type. So first we feed him—*her*—and then we see if we can coax her into the bathtub, and then, if your father agrees, tomorrow we'll take her over to the vet's and get her inoculations.''

"Great. I'm sure Dad will—"

"Whoa up, young lady. It's very probable that little Armand here isn't house-trained, and the first time he dirties on the carpet there's going to be trouble." Laurie stopped to stare at Sukie, who obviously didn't understand the magnitude of the problem. "So what we will do, little miss, is to divide this dog in two parts. I own the head and mouth, so I will feed her. You own the back half, so any time she dirties the rug you get to clean it up. Right?''

For a nine-year-old, Sukie Mason was a quick study. "You own the head?"

"Yes."

"So if she barks a lot it's your responsibility to quiet her down? And you have to feed her and stuff like that?''

"And stuff like that."

"And I own the back half—"

"Yes."

"And I have to walk her every day so she doesn't do do-do on the rug?''

"Right. Bargain?"

She could see the wheels go around in her head, ending up with a smile. "Right," Sukie said cheerfully. "So feed her.''

Laurie stretched up to the top shelf, where line after line of cat food held place of honor. "This is left from when Mimkie, my cat, was alive and I bought cat food by the case."

"But—but that's cat food."

"So she knows the difference?"

"No, I don't suppose she does, but—"

"But if you don't tell her she won't know, right?"

"Laurie Michelson, I think that's cheating. But I'll go along with it for two weeks, and we'll see."

"Now all you have to do is get your dad's permission, and you're home free."

The child groaned. "I knew there was some funny business in this somewhere. I have to catch my dad on a good day, right?"

"That's about it, love. Is this a good day?"

"I don't think so. He went out with a big scowl on his face."

And when he came back home the scowl was still there. He stomped into the living room, kicked off his shoes, and settled down into a big, over-stuffed chair. And groaned.

Laurie, who had not entirely forgotten the tired-man-comes-home-from-the-office drill, tiptoed around the edge of the room, concocted a bourbon and water and presented it to him with all the manners of an Egyptian slave girl. He slugged half of it down in one gulp, and then sighed. "Devil's own day," he muttered.

"More accidents?"

"No. More board meetings. You'd think we were asking for gold plating for the operating— What in hell is that?"

"That" sneaked her head around the corner of the door, made the distinction between male and female, and liked what she saw. Before a word of explanation could be expressed, Armand rushed across the room, barked twice in welcome, and stretched herself out on his stockinged feet.

"Great day in the morning!"

"As you say," Laurie murmured politely.

"Explanation!"

"For explanations you have to consult your daughter."

"You got it wrong," Sukie said as she romped into

the room. "Hi, Dad. I don't get to explain. The front end of her belongs to Laurie."

"What end?"

"The explanation end. She barked. Laurie owns all the front end of her. Her name is Armand. The dog, not Laurie."

"She has fleas." He shook one foot to dislodge his guest.

"Probably," Laurie commented. "But your daughter likes her. That ought to count for something."

Harry Mason admitted defeat and chucked the remainder of his drink down his throat.

"Maybe if you had another drink you'd see things in a better perspective," Laurie suggested hesitantly.

"And what does your mother say about the flea-bitten wreck?"

Laurie construed that to mean yes, whipped over to the bar in the corner of the room, and started mixing.

"Laurie's mama comed down the stairs and Armand tried to lick her hand, and she said, 'Oh, my goodness,' and then she turned around and ran up the stairs and she ain't come back down again."

"Smart woman, that one."

Silence bounced off the massive walls of the big house.

"Well, can we?" Sukie asked.

The dog rolled off Harry Mason's foot and collapsed, belly-up, pleading her own case with a few anxious whines.

"Oh, hell," Dr. Mason muttered. "Why me?"

"Because you're the man of the house now," Laurie said firmly. "It's in the contract. The man of the house always makes the decisions. Can we?"

"I don't know how I get into these things," he said explosively. "Yes, you can keep the mutt if I get my dinner in the next ten minutes. What are we having?"

"We got plenty of nice cat food," Sukie teased.

Her father glared at her, and pulled himself to his feet. "Yes," he growled. "I'm going to get a shower. Armand! Holy hell!" The dog, thinking she had been called, came to her feet and followed him up the stairs.

CHAPTER FIVE

"I DON'T care how many baths and inoculations that damn dog has," Harry Mason complained the next evening, "I'm not going to share my bed with her. Out, mutt!"

The dog grumbled, fell off the bed, and waddled out the open door.

Laurie scooted herself farther over in the bed...almost to the edge, for a fact. "Actually it's *my* bed, and you didn't hear me complaining when *you* got into *my* bed, did you?"

"Darn right," he muttered as he slammed the door behind him and pursued her. "And I better hadn't. I spent ninety-two thousand dollars on this house today. This house and everything under its roof!"

"I'm worth a darned sight more than that," she muttered. He extended a foot in her direction, landing it on the calf of her left leg. A cold foot. She struggled to suppress a shriek.

"Now what?"

"I'm also not a foot warmer," she objected. "Warm your feet before you come to bed."

"Yeah. How romantic."

"I don't remember anything in our contract about romantic." But you wish there were, her conscience told her. A whole lot more. There was something complex about her feelings for the doctor. When he frowned at her, it sent a cold shiver up her spine. When he smiled, there was a flash of light and contentment. And when he laughed she had to clasp her arms around herself to keep from breaking out in palpitations. Something complex? Or something stupid about myself? she wondered.

An arm came across her body and settled with one hand resting on her left breast. A large hand which squeezed gently and then settled with two fingers trapping her nipple.

"Soft," he said, chuckling. "That's what's so nice about squeezing a real woman."

"I wish you wouldn't do that," she muttered as she shifted a half-inch away from him...and promptly fell on the floor. "Darn," she said abruptly.

"This bed is wide enough for six," he said. She glared up at him. He had moved another inch or two, and was smiling down at her.

"I don't need all this," she said sarcastically. "I have three different classes tomorrow, and I bruise awfully easy. What are the students going to say if they look at my...at me...and see the bruises?"

"They'd better not say a word. Not a word. All you have to tell them is that you've just gotten engaged to be married, and you had a fine time." He reached down with one finger and tweaked her breast. "Now, if you'll get back in bed we will..."

Laurie rolled over on her stomach and then had another thought. "Will what?" she asked cautiously.

"We'll have a fine time."

She gradually pulled herself up onto her knees. Ralph had never done anything like this! Very suddenly it came to her that men were not all alike, and as she slowly pondered the thought he was out of the bed standing beside her. Standing in the soft glow of the bedside lamp.

And no, her eyes assured her, Ralph had hardly been like this at all. Neither was the statue of Hercules fighting the lion that stood in the open court of the university. What was it they called it? The rod of his wrath? Lord,

Harry Mason was endowed with enough for two. Men, that was, not wraths. And maybe too much for one. Woman, that was.

And by that time Harry had slipped his arm under her knees and picked her up off the floor. She gasped as he crushed her against his chest.

"Hurting you?"

"N-no," she gasped. Why tell him that his punishment was so delightful? He dropped a little kiss on her forehead as he carried her around the bed and tossed her gently into the middle of it.

"So there," he sighed as he released her.

"Yes," she murmured. "So there." She squirmed a little farther over, but not far enough before the mattress sank and he joined her.

"You don't...ever wear pajamas?"

"Not ever. It bothers you?"

"Well, yes," she said truthfully. "It...bothers me."

His left arm slipped under her shoulders. His right hand plucked open the nightgown that hid her breasts. He offered a little help to release them.

"You..."

"You what?"

"I...forget."

"It couldn't have been important, then; isn't that what they say?"

"I...don't know what they say. Ralph and I never really talked about such things."

"Poor girl."

His hand slowly drifted down the inner side of her breast and climbed up the other side to her stiffened nipple. A shiver went up her spine.

"You're like silk."

"Most women are." And she gave a sigh of pleasure as his hand coursed over the peak of her. "Put out the lamp. I'm not accustomed to...in the light, you know."

"I'm afraid I can't reach it. And I *am* accustomed to it."

By stretching as far as her arm would reach she managed to grab the lamp and pull its chain. There was a glimmer of moonlight through the open curtains.

Harry Mason said something. Laurie said something as well.

"I didn't know women cursed," he said.

"Some do." His hand was moving again, southward, for a fact, to a place more sensitive than her breast. She gasped. His hand stopped.

"This guy Ralph. How long were you married to him?"

"Three...three years, more or less. Why do you ask?"

"Three years? You don't seem to be...er...familiar with the drill?"

A large question mark at the end. He was bound to find out! Laurie bit her lip. It was not fear; it was shame.

"Something went wrong with the marriage?"

"I guess you could say that."

"Where is he now?"

"He was in Walpole Maximum Security Prison, up in Massachusetts," she whispered.

"That's one tough penitentiary up there."

She was glad that the light was out, but even so she ducked her head under the blankets. He gave her a little nudge. "Yes?"

"That's one of the toughest prisons in the state, that one. The parole board is a little loose, but going over the wall is pretty difficult."

"Yes, I know."

His hand left her body and tugged the blanket up. She felt bereft, missing the teasing hand.

"Well?"

"No, it's not very well." She bit her lip again to keep from crying.

"You might as well tell me. I'll find out anyway."

"Why do you have to know?"

"Because I want to know everything there is to know about you."

"Curse you!"

"So? He was in the maximum security prison in the Massachusetts prison system?"

"Yes."

"And under what sentence?"

"Take your pick. He did them all. Murder. Armed robbery. Dope smuggling."

"You didn't have to divorce him? What was the length of his sentence?"

"Life. They sentenced him to death, but the Governor commuted it to life. And I did divorce him. For wife and child abuse."

"You have a child?"

"Not any more. He murdered our two-year-old child, Dan."

"And when did all this terrible stuff take place?"

"Five years ago. He got mixed up with the New England Mafia. Ralph, he saw it as a great opportunity. He started off with the drugs and then expanded into the personal robberies. And then he broke his way out of the jail, and the state police caught him at it; later he swiped the cop-car and made his way to the West Coast.

"As far as Ralph was concerned, it was just a fine time. One year later he got involved in a Mafia fight between the Los Angeles and the San Diego organizations. Several men were killed, and Ralph was caught holding the bag, but he managed to escape again and came back home to me. He didn't know about the baby, but he decided that it wasn't his and he threw a coat over the boy...and then he slammed into me but the cops came just in time, and they took him to court and the Feds joined in and found him guilty of...of everything, and I divorced him."

"And that's why you're so nervous? Always looking behind you?"

She ducked her head and dabbed at her leaking eyes. "Yes. He haunts me."

"Well, don't worry. I'll look after you now."

"Thank you." It was barely whispered.

"I suppose he might have a lot of hatred toward you and your family?"

"Yes. As they dragged him out of the court he swore that he would get out, and that when he did he'd come after me. But I don't think he'd ever heard of this town. Well, I wasn't going to worry about it until I came to that bridge. I heard last year that he had been killed in a knife fight in prison."

He kissed her and enclosed her in his arms as she wept for her son, and the disaster she had made of her life. He cradled her in his arms until she fell asleep.

Early in the morning, he woke from a restless sleep. He rolled closer with both hands wrapped around her and infinite little passion points sprang to life where his hand had struck all the right places.

"I really am sleepy, Dr. Mason. I have three early-morning classes at the hospital, and— Don't do that. I can't sleep while you're doing all those kinds of things to me."

"Old Mother Nature," he assured her. "Once you turn on her engine there's no stopping the old girl."

"Stop that." She slapped at his wandering hands and missed, leaving a red mark on her own flat ivory stomach.

She whimpered at the self-inflicted pain, and railed at him. "Why don't you leave me alone, you...monster?" It was hard to work up a couple of tears, but she tried, and felt proud of herself as two big glossy globs dripped down each cheek. "See what you made me do?"

"Beautiful," he muttered softly, and he enclosed her

again in his arms, with one hand caressing her breasts as he kissed away the teardrops. "Relax and let me give you a taste of what is to come."

She gave up the struggle and gave herself into his loving care. A forbidden flash came to her. Ralph had never been so gentle or wonderful. The thought quickly vanished as she rose to meet his ardor and returned it in full measure.

"Mommy? Daddy? I'm cold."

There was a flurry in the middle of the bed as Harry Mason did his best to straighten out the sheets, while Laurie struggled to find the light switch, and the rest of her nightgown, and finally succeeded...with finding the nightgown, that was. But it took minutes for her to get into it.

"And what are you doing here in our bedroom, Sukie?"

"I couldn't sleep and it's cold and I heard you both talking..."

"Discussing," Laurie insisted. "We were discussing things...about marriage, you know. There are a million little problems that have to be solved to make a marriage run smoothly."

"Ha!" Not a pleasant sound from a nine-year-old daughter. "I'm cold."

Laurie looked over at Harry and shrugged. "Well, it's nice and warm here in our bed, so why don't you climb up and join us? Did you bring your bear?"

"I forgot my bear. I'll have to go get her. Save me a space."

"Yeah, save me a space." Her soon-to-be husband, Mr. McGrump, had piled a pair of pillows up behind his back and was sitting up, glaring at her.

"Well, she's only a little girl." Laurie went on the defensive. "She's in a new house, and a new neighborhood, and has a new set of parents. And in just a week she'll be entering a new school. The kid needs to be carefully chivvied along until she can make some adjustments.''

"And in the meantime I get to squeeze myself into a package and forget all about my libido?''

"No, darling, we were wonderful together.'' She kissed him and under her breath, "We must do it again soon.''

"When?''

"You're an adult,'' she reasoned gently. "You can surely restrain yourself this once in favor of your child? She is upset.''

"Yeah, sure.'' He rolled over, claiming all the blankets as he did so. "I don't have a shrink yet at the hospital. But when she arrives I'll probably need all her time to patch up this break in my mind.''

In a moment he was snoring. Fake or real, she could hardly tell. Loud, she was certain.

"I was only doing it for the good of the family,'' she told his back.

"Don't do me any more favors,'' he retorted. The snoring *was* fake. I'll get him in the morning for that, Laurie Michelson threatened. I will!

I'll get her in the morning, the good doctor also promised himself. The wedding will go off right after breakfast tomorrow! Darn if it won't! And from then on it'll be the devil take the hindmost!

Sukie was back in a flash...accompanied. The dog Armand was too small to vault to the high top of the bed, but a pair of assisting hands propelled her up and over until she landed squarely in the middle of the bed, where she burrowed into the warmest section and tried to appear necessary to the cause by licking the doctor's face.

"Darn dog,'' Harry muttered. "I'm trying to get some sleep!''

"It didn't seem so to me a few minutes ago,'' Laurie returned as she rolled over, her back to him, and pulled up the blankets. Sukie crawled over both of them and around the bed until she found a comfortable place between Laurie and her father. Armand whined a time or two and then coiled herself up next to the girl, who giggled as the dog licked her nose, and all of them fell into a restless sleep.

Two carpenters were still hammering away on the front stairs of the hospital when the Cadillac rolled up to the door the following day, crowded with people. The doctor drove. Maybelle, still half asleep, was running a constant complaint session while leaning against the car door. Laurie and Sukie sat in opposite corners of the back seat, glum-faced. "Why?" the little girl kept repeating. "Why?"

"Because Laurie and I are going to get married," her father snarled at her as he jammed on the brakes. The heavy car skidded in the dirt, raising a cloud of dust.

"You shouldn't do that," Laurie protested. "You'll ruin everything for all the patients."

"Aw, shut up," he responded grimly.

Laurie shrugged. "So much for love and happiness," she whispered to her prospective daughter. "Your father is a grouch!"

"Well, *I* knew that," the girl replied.

"But *I* didn't," Laurie said explosively.

"Then you should of looked more closely," Sukie muttered. "Or you could of asked. I could of told you, ya know."

"I'll bet you could," Laurie said, sighing. "Does my dress look all right?"

"Better 'n mine. I should of worn blue jeans."

"That's silly," Maybelle interjected from the front seat. "You wear bridal whites at a wedding. What did you do with my bottle, Laurie?"

"Left it at home on the kitchen table," Laurie said. "I don't plan to get married with a soused bridal attendant. Come to think of it, I don't plan to live with a drunken mother, either!''

"Well, it's about time," Dr. Mason snapped.

"Shut up," Laurie said pointedly.

"Yeah. Shut up," Sukie said.

"Well, really," Maybelle added as she turned her back on all of them.

"If anybody plans to attend this wedding you'd better get out," Harry Mason said. "I don't plan to drive any farther."

"I've gotta see what comes next," the child said as she flipped up the door lock and struggled out of the car.

"Me too," Laurie agreed. In a moment she and her prospective daughter were standing side by side, holding hands.

"How come you didn't wear a white dress?"

"This is as close as I could come," Laurie said. "It's a form of white. They call it ivory satin. It was all they had at the store." And then she asked, a little hesitantly, "Doesn't it look OK?"

"Yeah, it looks great, except for that stupid thing you've got on your head."

"They call that a veil. It's a sort of imitation veil, you know. Women are supposed to cover their hair in church. At least that's what the Bible says. I could take it off…"

"Don't bother on my account. Every female is allowed to look a little stupid once in a while."

"Thank you." It was not an enthusiastic "Thank you", as everyone noticed, but it was a form of politeness.

Sukie's father climbed out of the front seat and slammed the door.

"You look fine," he said as he took Laurie's arm at the elbow. "And as for you, young lady, no more remarks. None. You hear?"

"Or you'll beat me?" the girl asked, not the least perturbed by the threat.

"When did I last beat you?" her father demanded.

"Never," Sukie admitted. "But my mother made up for that. What happens next?"

"Are you all going to leave me sitting in this damned automobile?" Maybelle shrilled at them.

The two carpenters stopped carpentering, and moved to one side of the stairs. The double front doors to the hospital opened, and a band came out. Not a parade-size band, but four men and two women. The men carried kazoos. Nurse James, one of the women, played a big bass drum. Nurse Hart flashed a trumpet, and played with enthusiasm. It was obviously hard to play the Bridal March on a kazoo, so they compromised by working at "Amazing Grace".

"Rather well done," Laurie admitted cautiously. "Who is behind the trumpeter?"

"Dr. Ann Proctor. She joined us yesterday. Our psychologist, for a fact."

"She's pretty."

"Oh? I hadn't noticed."

"The hell you hadn't," Laurie whispered. Dr. Harry looked startled.

"The hell you say," he muttered.

"*Mommy,*" Sukie interjected, "you ain't supposed to use that word." Laurie was halfway through the door. "Have you been married before? Is that why you're wearing an ivory-colored dress?"

"Yes, dear."

"But you don't got no kids."

"Not from before," she answered quietly. "But now I've got you."

"Yeah." A very satisfactory comment. Sukie took Laurie's hand and held on tightly. "A second-hand bride?"

"So to speak."

"Daddy, did you know that Mama is a second-hand bride?"

"Yes, I knew. But I like her a whole bunch anyway. Let's go in. The chaplain is standing at the door, and he has more things to do than stand around in the cold breeze."

"Tell me *one* thing," Laurie whispered to him. She had a very low opinion of Chaplain Donohue. "Is he sober?"

"Not the two of you," Harry muttered. "One nag is enough."

"What are you two jabbering about?" Maybelle asked. "It's cold out here in the wind."

The band preceded them, still working on "Amazing Grace" as they went down the aisle, until a pump organ broke out in full splendor from the back of the room with the Bridal March.

"Dearly Beloved," Chaplain Donohue intoned, and Laurie and her daughter lost track of the proceedings, until the last words fell on Laurie's ear and the service was over.

It was announced, there was lunch and frivolity in the dining hall, and Laurie stood quietly amazed by the staff's congratulations. She knew most of them by name and medical profession, but not socially. And then Dr. Ann Proctor came over, and attempted to latch onto Harry's other arm.

"Not on your life," Laurie muttered as she clung desperately. Harry rocked back and forth under the pressure. "Hey," he whispered. "You're rocking the boat and I don't swim worth a plugged nickel."

"Don't tease me," she said, half in tears. "You're mine...mine!"

"I never knew you contemplated marriage," Ann said. "Again, that is."

"Well, I didn't, for a fact," he said heartily. "But then I met Laurie, and you know how that goes."

"I know," Ann said, shaking her head. "One step and you fall into the river. What's your specialty field, Laurie?"

"Oh, Laurie's not in the medical profession," Harry hastily interjected. "She's an actress. And...er...does a few lines now and then for our hospital training projects."

"Do you say so?"

"I do indeed."

Dr. Ann nibbled at her lower lip, and managed to look pleasantly unhappy. "What an interesting combination. I'll wager you have a hard time getting along with Suzanne."

"You mean Sukie? No, we don't have any trouble getting along together, do we, love?"

"Not yet, anyway," Sukie said, and gave them all a trouble-maker's smile. "I like this one." And therefore leaving everyone else to assume *they* were not among the favored few...

Now what have I done? Laurie's conscience screamed at her. He had a girlfriend all along. A doctor girlfriend! And I had to step into the middle of a line-up like that! That's like volunteering to be the target clown at the ducking stool!

It seemed that four times more guests had come to the buffet lunch than had attended the wedding ceremony. She mentioned the discrepancy to her mother.

"Oh, that always happens," Maybelle comforted her. "Freeloaders. People who are looking for the free drink. I see that your husband is well thought of in his profession."

"At the top of the ladder." Laurie could hardly avoid a jab. "Almost as important as a druggist, wouldn't you say?"

"Well, perhaps not *that* important, my dear. But if you put your shoulder to the wheel it would eventually mean a fine step upward. Where the devil are they hiding the good stuff?"

"I told the bartender to put it away after the first hour. We're not billionaires, you know."

"Spoilsport." Her mother hiccuped as she wandered toward the door. Laurie spent a minute counting to ten several times as she watched her mother stagger on her way. But there was no escape for Laurie Mason. Just as she felt the way was clear she felt a light hand descend on her arm.

"So tell me, Laurie," Dr. Ann inquired, "just how did you manage to snatch away one of the best prizes on the Southern marriage mart?"

"Snatch away?" Laurie managed a polite grin. "There he was, lying on the sidewalk in the gutter, all alone. Like a bird with a broken wing. Who could miss picking him up and nursing him to good health?"

The sweet, radiant face in front of her flushed. "Well, for your information, my dear, he was mine...all mine. I was called away to Europe for a social function, not expecting some wild Cherokee girl to snatch him away. Which only proves that one should never leave one's eggs unwatched!

"Oh, Harry, your lovely little wife was just explaining how she happened to fall in love with you. Sweet. Now tell me your side." And she snatched at the doctor's free arm and was steering him away into the crowd just as some enterprising soul found the switch to the automatic record player.

"And that shoots me dead," Laurie muttered.

Sukie, standing close by her—close enough still to have a cautionary finger on her new mama's dress—gave her a little tug. "She don't show well in mixed company," the child said. "But what did she mean by that wild Cherokee business?"

"Just a smart remark, love. Somehow or another she found out that I'm part Indian...of the Cherokee nation, for a fact. Does that make you feel bad—that your mother is part Indian?''

"Feel bad? It makes me feel good. Can you do a war dance?''

"Sukie! Certainly not here! In fact, I can hardly do any sort of a dance.''

"C'mon, Mom. Let's do a little dance together. You mustn't let some pale-face remark set you off. It's not that important.''

"Maybe,'' Laurie sighed, "but I haven't danced a single dance in the past six or seven years, and I suspect I just don't know how by this time.''

"Not to worry, Mama. I'll learn you.''

"Teach you,'' Laurie said.

"What?''

"Teach you, not learn you.''

"Heck,'' the child reflected. "I end up tied to an English teacher after all! But I'll learn you anyways. C'mon, old lady, they're playing a waltz.''

It might have been a waltz. At least the band was trying to play what might have been a waltz. But before Sukie could get in her licks her father appeared on the scene and claimed his wife.

"But this is my dance,'' the child insisted.

"Hey, girls don't dance with girls, love.''

"They do when there ain't no men around, and you was out playin' footsie with that blonde bimbo, and—''

"Watch your tongue, girl,'' her father said. "It's my wife, and my wedding, and we're going to dance first. Then you can have a turn.''

Sukie gave up. She shrugged like a young French girl, measured him for a quick kick in the ankle, and then changed her mind. "Did you know,'' she asked loudly enough to be heard over the band, "that you married an Indian girl?''

"Who, me?''

"Yes, you. Laurie's a Cherokee girl. An' you didn't even know it, did you?"

"No, can't say that I did. Why, is she planning to scalp me, or something?"

"She might. Indian women are fierce people. An' if you don't stop playin' around with that...that..."

"Blonde bimbo?" Laurie suggested.

"Exactly. With that blonde bimbo, who knows what just might happen?"

Sukie stamped her foot and wagged a finger at him, but Dr. Mason was not at all impressed. He swept Laurie up in his arms and navigated the floor to the tune of "The Vienna Waltz." Or something that seemed like that tune.

The good doctor was not exactly a skilled dancer but he was energetic. By the time they had circumnavigated the floor three times Laurie was puffing. "Do we have to be so...so enthusiastic?" she gasped.

"You'd better believe it. My daughter's watching, my secretary's standing there with her mouth open, and Dr. Proctor looks as if she's trying to find a scalpel in her purse. Are you really an Indian girl?"

"Really. Well, almost really. My great-great-grand-mother was a full-blooded Cherokee."

"And?"

"And us Indian girls, when we marry up, we don't share."

"Is that a threat?"

"You'd better believe it. Only don't tell my mother. As far as she's concerned we're both of us Georgia Belles. And don't step on my toe again, *Doctor*. I'm not the only one in this room who needs a little more practice!"

"Yes, well, I've had just too many surprises around here today."

"I can see that. You'll note that you and I are the only couple still dancing. The band quit about five minutes ago. And your daughter is over there staring at us with her thumb in her mouth. You'd better go over there and claim a dance with her.''

"That's silly. Men don't dance with children.''

"And women don't dance with little girls. People might think we had some sort of…problem.''

When he stopped dancing the audience applauded. So he bowed to them all, pulled Laurie tight up against him, and kissed her on her forehead.

"Just wait until I get you home,'' he murmured in her ear. "Just wait!''

"I'm trembling in fear,'' she countered saucily. "I can hardly wait.'' And she stepped away from him and curtsied. "Don't wear yourself out in the meantime.''

"C'mon, Dad, it's my turn.'' And the pair of Masons swirled away from her in a dance whose name Laurie didn't even know. She settled back on her heels and caught a deep breath.

"You'll be sorry,'' a voice beside her said. "You'll be darn well sorry.'' Laurie looked around. Dr. Ann Proctor was standing at her side, tapping an impatient finger on the top of her tiny purse. "And very soon, too.''

Laurie's nose was itching. She raised a hand to scratch at it. The old New England phrase struck her. Have a fight or kiss a fool! She stared at the blonde bimbo. "You may be right,'' she said, sighing. "You may very well be right!''

And that was the very time when the doctor and his daughter whirled back to them and made a classic gliding stop. "Time to go home,'' he announced, breathing a little heavily from the exercise.

"Oh, the very thing!'' Dr. Proctor exclaimed. "I came without my car, Harry. Do you suppose…?''

"A drive home, Ann? Of course.'' He reached out to take her arm. "We Masons would be happy to oblige.''

Sukie moved to her new mother's side and twitched

at her dress to get attention. "The hell we would," the child muttered. "That's like inviting a pair of rattlesnakes into the parlor."

"Sukie!"

"Well, it's true, isn't it?"

"True, I don't doubt," Laurie whispered back. "But a girl your age shouldn't use that sort of language."

"Ha!"

"Ha?"

"You hafta learn the language if you're gonna be a Mason. And we'd better hurry up if we want to ride home ourselves."

Laurie turned around to look. The two doctors were already halfway to the doors, both chattering away in that peculiar language that medicine people used among themselves.

"When you're right you're right," Laurie said to the child as she grabbed Sukie's arm and towed her across the dance floor, remembering that her coach might turn back into a pumpkin at the stroke of the hour.

CHAPTER SIX

LAURIE came home from the hospital early on Friday, a week after the wedding. The house was quiet. Sukie was in her new school and not sure that she liked it. Maybelle was upstairs in her room, snoring away. And Harry? Harry was still tied up at the hospital. Another emergency operation. An orthopedic case resulting from a three-car accident on Pearl Street.

So Laurie brushed Armand the dog out of her favorite chair, mixed herself a non-alcoholic drink, and fell back into the chair with her feet up. It had been a hard day.

The front door banged. She consulted her watch. One o'clock? Too early for Sukie to be coming home. But it *was* the little girl, dragging her backpack along the floor behind her, wearing a face too long for her age, and a skirt too short for the same.

"What's the trouble, love?"

"Oh, I—" And then she collapsed. The child abandoned her pack, pushed her dog aside, and with a riot of tears flushing out her eyes threw herself across the room and onto Laurie's lap. Laurie, with a heart full of sympathy, gathered her up and cuddled her close.

"What's the trouble, love?"

"They hate me at that school."

"Oh? Tell me about it."

"They all laughed at me this morning."

"Why would they do that?"

"Because they was all jealous. They yelled that I was runnin' around half-naked, and then they caught me in a circle and pulled at my hair and threw chalk an' erasers at me, and…''

''And the teacher?''

''Mrs. Wilson. She wasn't there until after the bell rang, and then—''

''And then?''

''And then Billy Bledler, the big kid, he said my dad was a pill-pusher and my mother was a oar, and I didn't know what that all meant so I punched him in his belly and he fell down on the floor and it felt so good hittin' him that I kicked him a couple of times and…broke his glasses, and that's when Mrs. Wilson came in.'' She stopped to take a deep breath.

''And then they sent me to the office, and I had to sit in an old rickety chair in the hall, and then…'' There was another pause, for tears of anger this time. ''Nobody's gonna call my dad a pill-pusher. Nobody.''

''Yes, I can see that. And then?''

''And then the principal gived me a note and sended me home.'' She stopped to wipe her eyes. ''And that's all.''

''And that seems to be enough for one day,'' Laurie murmured. ''Where's the note?''

''I…I thought it would make you mad, so I throwed it down the sewer. And Mrs. Wilson saw me and said she was gonna call you tonight!''

Sukie stopped crying and sat up. ''You ain't really mad at me, are you, Laurie?''

''No, not really.'' Laurie sighed. ''It's hard to be a lady these days, isn't it? Why don't we go out in the kitchen and try it out on cookies and milk?''

''Cookies? Store-boughten?''

''Made them myself,'' Laurie boasted as she took the child's hand and led her back to the kitchen, where she sat Sukie down at the table and went to the refrigerator to take out the milk.

''Choc'late chip? My favorite.''

"Thank God for that, they're the only sort of cookies I know how to make!"

"I don't believe that, Mama. I bet you can make ten different kinds of cookies, whenever you want to."

"Keep talking, child. Flattery will get you everywhere." Sukie gave her a wide-mouthed grin and started on the glass of milk Laurie had given her. It was easy to read the little girl's face. "Nobody's gonna call my dad a pill-pusher." And her mother is "a oar"? What the devil could the boy have meant by that? Laurie wondered. And the only boat I've ever been on was the replica of the *Mayflower*, up in Plymouth Harbor in Massachusetts. And as far as I can remember there weren't any oars... Oar? Could they mean...? Good Lord! All those children are too young for *that* kind of conversation, aren't they?

Sukie called for another glass of milk, and was reaching for the last cookie on the plate when Harry Mason came into the room. "Hey, cookies? I'll have a half dozen..."

"That's the last one," his daughter informed him solemnly. "Not a single one left." Her quick hand covered the only cookie left on the dish.

"Well, now," he said, showing a long face. "Well, now. And what are you doing at home at this time of day, young lady?" And so Sukie told him, holding nothing back, but having trouble with a stray tear or two.

"And this boy called your mother a what?"

So Sukie went back over the story, emphasizing "pill-pusher," but running quickly over oar. Her father gave a one-handed stop sign as Laurie got up to pour him a cup of coffee.

"Pill-pusher," he mused. "A common term used for medical people. You can't insult a doctor with that. But this other?"

Sukie repeated herself, and then watched anxiously as

her father's face clouded over. "Like in a boat," the child added.

"Yes, I see." There was another pause. "Well, I came home early because I have to make a trip down to Atlanta. An emergency meeting of the area medical council. So you, young lady, start your homework while your mother comes upstairs to help me pack."

And before Laurie could add a word to the subject she found herself halfway up the stairs, with one hand gripped ever so securely in the muscular hand of the doctor. Who said not a word until the bedroom door closed behind them. And he flipped the lock on the door.

"What in the world...?"

And then he tossed her into the middle of the massive bed.

"Watch it! You could hurt a girl with a move like that." She stared up at him speculatively, and then tugged her skirt back to knee level.

"Not a brawny thing like you," he said, chuckling. He sat down on the edge of the bed, and in seconds his shoes, socks and trousers were gone.

"But..."

"It just struck me that I could drive all the way down to Atlanta, and get in an accident, and miss all the fun and cheer of a lifetime." His shirt fell on the floor and he crawled across the mattress until he was close beside her.

"So you...?"

"So I thought I'd take advantage of this lovely afternoon." The buttons on her blouse came apart, except for the top one. "Darn!" He snapped it off with his surgeon's fingers. "And then..." Her skirt came unzipped, and her bra fell by the wayside.

Laurie, struggling for a sensible comment, could not find one. "But I'll catch a cold," she sighed. "I need a bra to..."

"No, you don't." Both of his big hands came up and

covered her full breasts. ''Not any more, you won't, now
that you've got a husband. That's what husbands are for,
you know. And for things like this.'' His hands shifted
and her briefs disappeared. ''See?''

Laurie was beginning to see. Although her first husband had never been much more than a prize in a cracker
box, he'd known some things that were evidently uni-
versal in the male world. Dr. Harry Mason had obviously
been to the same school but had learned more. His left
hand lingered on her curly mound of Venus, while his
right marched smartly back up to her breast and...

''What are you doing?'' she said frantically as all her
nerves responded. Slowly at first—it had been a long
time—and then at high speed.

''You don't know?''

''I...I'm not sure. We were going to have a...''

''A good time before I go to Atlanta.''

Laurie wanted to say something important. Unfortunately, she couldn't remember what it was. But when he
rolled on top of her the whole thing came back in a flash.
From that moment she was lost.

Several minutes later...which seemed like hours...out
of breath, bearing his whole weight on her frail
body...with pleasure...she asked, ''I thought we weren't
going to do this sort of thing? You said...''

''No, you said.''

''And you didn't agree?''

''At the time it wasn't important and I was too busy
at the hospital straightening things out and catching up
on the backlog of operations needing to get done.''

''And now it is?''

''And now it is. It struck me that raising Sukie all by
herself would not be as good as having two. Don't you
think?''

''I...I'm not sure.'' She shuddered and steeled herself.
If there was to be a companion for Sukie in this family,
then there would have to be a certain amount of...sexual

relations...between her and her husband. And not just once, for goodness' sakes. It would require several encounters, to say the least. She swallowed hard.

"Then let's try it again, and maybe you'll make up your mind."

"You can do it twice?"

"I don't want to boast, but, over a short period of time, yes."

Good Lord! Find an excuse! "I...don't have any protection."

Harry said, "Think of it this way: procreation is recreation—and you didn't have any the first and second time we made love."

"Oh," Laurie answered.

"Now stop wiggling around. My aim is not as good as it ought to be."

But it was, and until Sukie came up and knocked on their door he proved, adequately, that he was a multistar performer. But Laurie's experience in the marriage game had left her somewhat short of understanding. Her previous husband had been one of those quick slam-bang-thank-you-ma'am performers, and Harry had already demonstrated that he was far above and beyond that limitation!

"Does it always have to be so...quick?" she asked. And that proved something. In her first marriage she wouldn't have dared to ask!

Sukie banged on the bedroom door with more enthusiasm than common sense. The good doctor sighed, but ducked his responsibility. Laurie moved into the breach.

"What is it, love?"

"That hospital lady is sittin' outside in her car and blowin' the horn, and she waked Grandma up and she's mad. Daddy?"

"Daddy's asleep, love." He wasn't, but he did look a little green around the gills, and he *had* been working hard. "What hospital lady is that?"

"You know, Mama. The blonde bimbo."

"Oh, my!" She shook Harry's shoulder urgently, until he managed to get one eye open. "There's someone at the door, blowing her horn and asking for you." Both of his eyes came open.

"Tell her...tell them... Whoever is it?"

"Beats me, love. It sounds like it might be the blonde bimbo."

"Dr. Proctor?"

"Sounds like it."

"Oh, fiddle, I must have overslept. I'll slip into a robe and..."

"Don't be silly. You're all over-sweat and under-enthusiasm. Go take a shower. I think you overextended yourself. I'll go down and beard the lion. Lioness. Do female lions have beards?"

"I don't know. Overextended myself? Fat chance. I could do it again right now."

"I'm sure you could, love. You are certainly well equipped for this, but you could get a hernia as well. Scoot, boy. Playtime is over."

Laurie slid off the bottom of the bed and snatched up her robe. "She's going to Atlanta with you?"

"Yes. Didn't I tell you?"

"Slipped your mind, I guess, lover." But you and I will have time to talk this over later, husband, she thought. I'm jealous, aren't I? But why? This was meant to be a marriage of convenience, and all of a sudden I've got nervous twinges all over my body just because you're playing around with a blonde bimbo! I can't seem to settle down and do right about the world. And not only am I jealous of my husband, but I've certainly fallen in love with my little girl! Is there a bigger fool in the family than me?

She shook out her mess of curls and gave a saucy wiggle of her posterior in his direction, and Mrs. Harry

Mason went off to fight dragons...or witches—which-ever.

"You're not really dressed, Mama." Sukie paused at the head of the stairs and reached out for Laurie's hand.

"I'm dressed, love, with bra and panties. Don't you like my morning coat?"

"But it's afternoon. And it's got a lot of lace and stuff, and you can see through it in the sunlight. What do you think the doctor lady is going to say when she sees you like that?"

"I'm eager to find out, sweetheart. Remind me to stand in the sunlight when I get down to the lounge. And now run ahead and tell the good doctor that I'll be along in just a second."

At nine years of age Sukie was nobody's fool. She gave Laurie a solemn searching look, dropped her hand, and skipped down the stairs, both cheeks dimpling as she struggled to keep from laughing. At the bottom step she stopped, grabbed at the banister and turned her little face back up toward Laurie. "You are some kind of a cake, Mama," she called, and fled toward the front door.

"Yes," murmured Laurie Mason. "But the question is, what kind...?"

She struggled at low speed down the stairs. As a result, Miss Ann Proctor was sitting uncomfortably in one of the worn, over-stuffed chairs in the lounge, tapping her foot, looking around as if the mediocre furnishings were upsetting her stomach.

"Ah, at last," the blonde said. "I wouldn't have thought it would take you so long to put on so little."

"Probably not," Laurie sighed. "But I'm so...I lack experience with dogs and children and husbands. And Harry, he has this odd habit. He waits until I'm fully dressed, and then he demands that we...well... And then I have to get all undressed again, and...it is difficult, as I'm sure you must realize?"

Sukie giggled. Laurie gave her a dirty look.

"I'm afraid I don't know anything at all about whatever it is you're talking about," Dr. Proctor said disdainfully. "Will Harry be long?"

"Nobody would know," Laurie murmured. "Harry does what Harry wants when Harry wants it. I'm sure you must know from experience?"

Dr. Proctor had the grace to blush. So did Laurie. It wasn't what she had meant to say, but, standing behind their visitor, Sukie was making thumbs-up signs like crazy. And before anyone could say anything else Maybelle Michelson wandered into the room, thumping heavily on her cane.

"Laurie," her mother snapped. "At least you could have had the courtesy to tell me we had a visitor."

"We don't, really," Laurie returned. "This is Dr. Proctor, from the hospital. She's here to see Harry."

"Oh," Maybelle remarked, losing all attention. "One of the employees? I wish he would hold all his meetings in his office. I can't find that bottle of zinfandel."

"No, I suspect not," Laurie sighed. "Somebody drank it all last night, and we don't have another bottle to our…"

And Harry came down the stairs. Conversation stopped.

"Well, ladies," he said, in a jovial mood. And how does he do that, Laurie asked herself. I was sure he was worn down to the nub, and here he is full of good cheer. And a conversation-stopper if ever there was one.

"About ready to go?" Ann Proctor chortled. It sounded as if she was prepared to wait any number of days if the great man wasn't quite ready. Harry waved a hand, as if time were irrelevant. And then Maybelle joined the chase.

"Proctor? Did I hear you say Proctor?"

A cautious "Yes, ma'am" came from the doctor.

"Knew a Proctor family some years ago. Started out

on the wrong side of the tracks, and worked their ways up. Your folks?''

''I guess.''

''Had a terrible bad habit. Never paid their bills. Made my husband so mad. 'Like pills come two for a penny,' he used to say. One of the girls got to be a schoolteacher. Married into the Wilson family, I heard.''

''My sister,'' Ann Proctor said.

''Yes? Greatest gossip in the state. Troublemaker. Uses her tongue as a weapon.''

''My teacher is named Mrs. Wilson,'' Sukie contributed. ''Hates half-breeds. When I told her my new ma was Cherokee she made me sit across the room so's nobody else could catch it.''

''Being a Cherokee is not something you can catch, Sukie,'' her father admonished. ''There was a time when the Cherokee nation owned all the land from the mountains here to the big river.''

''Mississippi River,'' Laurie interpreted for the abashed Dr. Proctor.

''Time for us to go,'' the young blonde interjected.

Harry slowly pulled a gold watch out of his vest pocket. ''You're so right,'' he said. ''But just one more time, Sukie, I want to hear what the kids were calling us in class today.''

''You mean like pill-pusher?''

''Yes, and what about your mother?''

''They said she's a oar. That's when I hit Billy Bledler. And I got punished for startin' a riot. They can't talk about my mother and father that way. Can they, Dad?''

Somebody in the room was crying. Sobbing. Or maybe, Laurie thought, it's not that at all. She managed to pull her attention away from Harry and the blonde bimbo. It was neither of them; it was the doyenne of town society—her own mother. And Maybelle was laughing, not crying.

"She has appealed to Caesar," Maybelle said wistfully, "and to Caesar she must go."

"What's that mean?" Sukie asked, half-terrorized by the atmosphere between the other two.

"Not important," Laurie said. "It means your dad will take care of it all."

And with that positive assurance the little girl threw herself across the room and into Laurie's lap, half crying, half laughing, but at all times clinging with all her strength.

Laurie settled back in her chair, holding the child tenderly, guarding the little one's fears with her adult concern, only... "Is that true, Harry?" she asked. Caesar hadn't pontificated in the past two or three weeks.

"That's true," Harry Mason said. "I'll take care of this little mess. But we are getting late, Ann. Let's get going. We can talk about this argument, and...your cousin, is it?...on our drive to Atlanta."

"Sister, not cousin," Maybelle interjected, bringing the sin and the sinner closer together.

The pair of them moved swiftly up out of their chairs, heading for the door, with faces shaded like a thin slate of tin, and yet trying to smile just the slightest. Dr. Proctor was trying hard to be happy, but left behind her the feeling of a woman preparing for the guillotine.

Silence—a friendly silence—filled the room, while outside there was a feeling of doom and destruction. The car motor roared, the tires skidded in the loose sand of the yard, and everything was quiet.

"Everybody breathe deeply," Laurie commanded. Everyone complied. One, two, three, four deep breaths.

"And now everyone into the kitchen. Blueberry doughnuts. Won't take but a minute to fix 'em." She was greeted by a charged shout from everyone but Maybelle.

"I do know where there's half a bottle of Chardonnay," Laurie coaxed. "But only one." It was enough to put a smile on the face of the oldest resident, and so they went trouping off to the kitchen, with Armand bringing up the rear.

"Now what was that all about?" Maybelle sagged into the strongest kitchen chair and waited.

"Well, briefly, Sukie had some trouble at school. Some kids called her a few things that don't fit in children's vocabularies. And then we discovered that Dr. Proctor is the sister of the teacher of this class."

"Ah."

"Yes, 'ah'. It would appear that an adult gossip was mixed up in the whole procedure."

"Ah," Maybelle said again. "Now, about that wine bottle you were telling me about…?"

Laurie concentrated on making the doughnuts. It wasn't really true that she knew nothing about kitchens. While attending school in Boston she had worked on the night shift at the local doughnut shop. And so she mixed and churned and kneaded, half the time with her eye on her mother. Maybelle had not always been a boozer. Not until she'd run out of money had she turned to the bottle. The cellar had been filled with wine then. And now she was sitting by the bottle of wine, fingering it, but not making a single effort to uncap the bottle.

The front doorbell rang. Sukie slid down from her chair and ran to answer. A moment later she was back. "The Harrington kids," she announced. "Do I have time to play with them…until the doughnuts are ready?"

"No reason why not," Laurie assured her. "I'll make a batch for the grown-ups, and then another for you kids. Scoot you go."

Sukie left with a whoop.

"The child," Mrs Michelson said, "she's happier than she was when she first came. Don't you think?"

Laurie paused, resting her hands on her rolling pin. "Yes, I think you're right, Mother."

"And you?"

"I'm...happier than I was before. I don't seem to have nightmares so often. And you, Mother?"

"I can't tell you what a relief it is to have a roof over our heads, and the mortgage paid. And your husband is a fine man, even though he's only a surgeon."

Laurie chuckled. "*Only* a surgeon? That's the highest ranking in the hospital pecking order."

"Do you say so? Not as high as a chemist, my dear. Nobody outranked your father. Nobody!"

"I suppose you're right." Laurie knew better, but the fight wasn't worth the candle. If her mother thought chemists were the top of the tree, then why should her daughter make a fight out of it?

And just at that moment a small scream was raised from out in back of the house, and then amplified by a couple more voices, and Laurie Mason was out the back door, barefoot, like a whippet. Sukie met her a dozen steps down the hill, pointing to the pool behind the hill.

"The boys," the child shouted. "I didn't know they couldn't swim." All the noise was concentrated in the center of the large, Olympic-size swimming pool. A mad splashing in the middle of the pool, coupled with large shouts for help, pinpointed the area of the problem. The two younger Harrington boys had fallen off the little rubber lounger, struggled to regain a hold, and then separated, the younger drifting north, the older splashing his way south, closer to the edge.

With one quick glance Laurie assessed the situation, slid to a stop just long enough to shed her robe, and plunged into the water in a racing dive. Behind her, Sukie raced around the edge to the nearest point where the older boy, Neil, was still struggling, and she too plunged into the cold water. Laurie raised her head just long enough to measure the girl's progress, and then, satisfied, rolled into an Australian crawl, heading for the panic-stricken younger child.

The boy snatched at her head, pulling her under the

water. It had been a long time since Laurie had practiced her life-saving techniques, but in her youth she had won the state lifesaving contest three times. Courage and method came back to her in seconds. She flipped the boy over on his back, settled herself beneath him, clasped one arm across the child, and then began a strong backstroke and began talking to Sean, encouraging him.

Gradually his panic subsided, and he lay still in the water, moving only as she coaxed and towed him. In a matter of minutes she grounded on the edge and staggered out of the water, dragging the boy behind her. She flipped him over and began pumping water out of his lungs.

One hundred yards away Sukie had already beached the older boy. And in those two or three minutes someone in the house had dialed the 911 emergency number, and a siren heralded the arrival of the rescue squad...and the mobile truck of WFTA television...and a car from the *Grandell Daily News*.

The car arrived first. In fact, the two photographers from the newspaper were standing knee-deep in the water, snapping shots of Sukie...but not exactly helping.

"Help her, you idiots," Laurie screamed. "She's only nine years old!"

Interest stirred. The photographers reloaded. The television crew pushed their way to the front of things and filled the area with their floodlights. Finally the rescue squads set up shop, and the two waterlogged boys were taken in hand.

A crowd had gathered to see what was happening. The Harringtons puffed their way up the hill to see what the excitement was all about. A neighbor told them, "Hey, I think that's your two youngest boys that are being taken to the ambulance."

Bill Harrington pushed and shoved and demanded to be let through. "Those are my boys that are injured."

Rose, with an ashen face, followed in his footsteps. "Please let me see my boys," she pleaded.

The policeman noticed their struggles. "Take it easy now, folks," he said as he broke a path for them.

"They're all right now." Sukie met them at the ambulance, wringing her hands as the tears dropped one by one down her cheek. "I didn't know they couldn't swim. I am so sorry."

Bill patted her on the head. "Now, now," he said as he anxiously looked at his sons being carried into the ambulance.

"If you are the boys' parents, they are doing fine now, thanks to this girl and her mother," the paramedic explained to them. "We are taking them in for a checkup. One of you can travel with the boys."

"Mother, you get in," Bill said, pushing her toward the door. "I'll get the car and our medical insurance cards and will meet you at the hospital. Don't worry too much," he added as he gave her a hard squeeze. "Boys will be boys."

He noticed Laurie was collapsed on the ground, all alone. "Sukie, you go join your mother; she needs you." He gave her a small push to start her off.

Laurie rocked with her arms around her knees, hugging herself. Oh, God, suppose the boys had drowned? Even in spite of the fence and locked gate, they'd managed to get in. Who would have thought, with the cold water, anyone would go near it? Of course adventuresome boys would. She shivered from the chilly water.

Maybelle used her heavy malacca cane to beat a passage through to Laurie's side. "Get up, and let me put this coat on you. You're indecent in your underclothes and nothing else on," she commented strongly as she helped her into her old dark navy blue raincoat. "I hope those picture-taking men didn't get any of you. They sure look as if they are more interested in you than the boys."

"Were there any photographers here?" She was too exhausted to care at that moment. She started to shudder with the cold.

The crowd regathered as the ambulance left and surrounded Maybelle, Laurie and Sukie, all asking questions at once.

She couldn't hear a word. "Oh, my word." She suddenly realized they were taking pictures of all of them. She turned her back to the cameras and, taking her mother and Sukie's hands, started pulling them out of the crowd, only to find her way blocked. Policeman Jake, an old friend of the family, taking pity on them, stepped in and started to make a path up the hill. Several video and cameramen got whacked on the shins with Maybelle's cane for their efforts at trying to crowd in.

Sukie and Laurie's teeth were chattering, and they were both shivering. Maybelle thanked Policeman Jake and asked, "Can you get this crowd off the premises?"

"Yes, Miss Maybelle." He turned and started shooing the crowd out the driveway.

With Laurie and Sukie wrapped in blankets, Maybelle pushed them up the stairs, locked the door and ran hot baths for both of them. She stripped Sukie and got her into the tub. "Laurie, aren't you undressed yet?" Shaking her shoulders, she ordered, "Get out of this coat and hurry up into the tub."

Laurie was half asleep. "What's the matter?" she croaked, dragging herself out of the chair. "I want to get into bed and get warmed up."

"You'll warm up faster in the hot tub than in bed. Hurry up," she said as she pushed Laurie into the steaming bathroom.

"Yes, Mother." She stepped into the tub. "Oh! This feels so good, like heaven should." She moaned. "Heat is wonderfully warm." Her eyes started to close.

Again Maybelle shook her shoulders. "Wake up, wake up; I can't do you and Sukie at the same time.

You are not to drown while I get her dried and dressed. You hear me?''

"Yes, Mother," she murmured.

Maybelle hadn't worked so hard in years. She dried Sukie with a good rubdown and then got her into fresh jeans, shirt and a sweatshirt. "At least you are more cooperative than your mother. Now to get her out before she turns into a prune."

"I don't want to move," Laurie complained as her mother grabbed her chin and hair and pulled. "Ouch, that hurts!" And she erupted like a geyser, slipping and sliding on the bottom of the tub, trying to get her balance, splashing water in all directions, soaking Maybelle. Laurie grabbed the towel bar. It came off the wall, plunking her again to the bottom of the tub, releasing a wave of water onto the floor.

"Oh, you have soaked me with your antics. Look at me!" cried Maybelle. "Now I have to change all my clothes too. Are you awake, so I can leave you?"

"Yes, Mother" came Laurie's contrite reply. "I'm fully awake now. Although sleeping through this nightmare would have been a blessing."

CHAPTER SEVEN

"WELL," Maybelle Michelson said as she lazed back in her chair and savored the drink her daughter had brought. "We certainly showed them, didn't we?" She took a sip. "My Lord, what did you put in this?"

"It's a diet soft drink," Laurie said. She and Sukie were cuddled up together in the big armchair, surrounded by blankets, eyes on the television set, while drinking hot chocolate in mugs. "If you want, I can get you some hot chocolate instead."

Her mother glared at her. "Have we run out of wine?"

"Yes, we are fresh out." Laurie started to cringe as the news came on, showing her in her wet bra and panties as she worked on Sean. She rocked back and forth on her knees, pumping the water out of his lungs. Her wet bra was no cover and her breasts were prominently displayed to all the viewing public. She felt herself turning red as a tomato and, inwardly shrinking, she groaned. Fortunately, her back was turned as she collapsed on the ground, but the view as she stood while Maybelle helped her put on her raincoat— "Oh! Sweep me up to heaven or hide me in a dark closet," she cried.

"Why didn't they show me? I hauled Neil out of the water," an insulted Sukie asked.

"Well, dear, they did show you talking to the boys' parents."

"At least you were decently clothed," Laurie murmured under her breath. Sukie heard her.

"Your bikini looks the same doesn't it? Ah! At least I think so." So pondering, she shook her head questioningly.

"If your father sees this newscast, he will believe everything that blonde bimbo Proctor has told him." She felt despair, and unease. What will he think? she wondered. This afternoon was so wonderful, I felt like I was really married.

"Which reminds me, young lady." She turned and glared at Sukie. "How did you and the boys get into the pool area? That's a very tall fence to climb and the gate was locked. Wasn't it?"

Head hanging down, Sukie said, "Well, Neil said I was a wimp if I didn't get the key so they could see the pool close up. So I got the key and unlocked the gate." She glanced up to test Laurie's reaction. "I only meant for them to walk around the pool, but when we reached the middle Neil saw your chair-lounger afloat. He and Sean jumped on it before I could stop them."

Sukie was crying now. "I know you said no one was to go in the pool without you there," she said as she buried her head in Laurie's lap. "Honest I didn't know they would jump in. I only meant to show them around."

Laurie patted her on the back and found her napkin to help dry her tears. "At least you did the right thing in calling for help right away and aided Neil out of the water." Laurie thought, She is punished enough with fright, but I will have to reprimand her for disobedience. "You know, I did tell you that you were not to enter the pool area without permission nor go into the pool without me or your father being there. What shall I do to punish you for disobedience?" She paused and looked at the downcast head burring in her lap. "What does your daddy do when you are this naughty?"

"He sits me in his lap and lectures me on what I did

and how a lady should act. But I don't think it does much good. I'm not old enough to be a lady.''

Laurie had a hard time covering a grin. The corners of her mouth twitched.

"Well, we will have to think of something. First, when the Harringtons get home, you and I will have to go there. You will have to apologize to them, and let the boys know the rules of the house. No climbing. No opening the gate. No entering the pool without an adult there. Do we understand each other clearly?''

Sukie nodded. "Yes.''

"To help, I will get Buddy, Delia's husband, to put the winter cover over the pool. I should have had it put on earlier, but with all the confusion around here I forgot. When your father comes home, you will have to explain what happened.''

Sobbing loudly, Sukie buried her head in Laurie's shoulder.

Maybelle's voice was raised as she answered the phone. "No one is home and I can't hear what you are saying,'' she said as she slammed the phone on its hook. The bell rang again and she repeated herself twice more. Laurie hopped up, dumping Sukie on the floor. She took the receiver from her mother as the phone rang again.

"Hello?'' She turned green, then red, and then ashen, slamming down the phone. Turning to her mother, she asked, "Is that the kind of filth you heard?'' Maybelle nodded as she hunted and found half a bottle of wine and poured herself a drink. The phone rang again. Laurie lifted the receiver, heard two words, hung up and four seconds later dropped it and left it hanging on its cord.

"Does anyone want any supper?'' She left the question hanging in the air as she clutched her head with both hands. "I have a splitting headache. Help yourselves,'' she mumbled, and started staggering to the stairs.

"You do that. Sukie and I can take care of ourselves. I will bring you some hot tea and aspirin."

Whatever the noise was, Laurie knocked over her alarm clock and the telephone onto the floor without opening her hazel eyes. She pressed both hands to her head, groaning. Her head ached. Oh, for the oblivion of sleep again.

Her opened window let in the scent of fall with a cold breeze. Leaves, flowers and shrubs decaying and hibernating with the early touch of cold. The chirping birds were trying to get their fill before winter set in. Small flocks were getting started for their trip to South America and parts unknown. She covered her ears to drown out the sounds and then she heard the stairs creak and two voices whispering. Her door squealed open in spite of the effort to open it quietly.

"What do you want?" her croaking voice queried.

"We wondered if the phone woke you up and if you'd like breakfast in bed." Maybelle, Sukie and Armand were there to comfort her. Armand tried licking her face in sympathy.

"Oh, no. Just tea and aspirin. I feel sick."

"Dear child, where do you hurt?" This reminded her of the time she'd had measles and her mother had helped take care of her. It felt good to be cocooned in her mother's love, instead of her having to soothe her mother's woes.

"Head," was her reply. Eyes still closed, she asked, "Who hung up the phone?"

"I did," came Sukie's abashed voice. "I thought Daddy might be trying to talk to us, especially if he saw the news report last night or this morning."

Laurie's bleary red eyes popped open. "I don't really need this," she moaned, hanging onto her head. "You'd better give me a double dose of aspirin followed by a cup of tea. Please don't hang up the phone; my head won't stop going around and hurting. I can't see straight either.''

''You have a good migraine.'' Maybelle hustled out to her medicine cabinet.

At noon, Laurie rose to greet the remainder of the day. Her headache was almost gone, if she didn't turn her head too quickly. She walked very cautiously down the stairs, only to be greeted by Sukie tackling her and knocking her back on the stairs.

''Oh, please, dear. Don't rattle me; I may fall apart. My equilibrium is way off today. Handle me with care, love.''

''What's ekeliebem?''

Maybelle pulled her off Laurie. ''It means balance. Try talking softly. No slamming doors and leave the phone off the hook for the rest of the day. This should restore our equilibrium.

''Laurie,'' her mother added as she helped her to her feet, ''why don't you stay in bed for today? I called and you have no classes. We also have a pack of rats at the gates which you don't want to see. Officer Jake said he would keep them in hand and his father said he would come and relieve him. Says he's got his shotgun loaded with rock salt, if they try to bother me. That's real nice of him.'' Maybelle preened. ''One time, he came court-ing and he still remembers.''

''Grandma, do you mean that old man that sits on the park square bench talking all day?''

''You mind your p's and q's, gal. Someday you will be my age and remembering when all the boys were sparking you. It's pretty nice to know they remember you at my age.

''Now upstairs with you, Laurie. Sukie, help your mom upstairs and into bed. I will bring you some broth and tea in a few moments.''

Laurie slept most of the day and night away after eat-ing and taking some pills.

"This is more like it," she declared when she woke, and she yawned, stretched and listened to the birds calling to each other. "Oh, this should be Sunday and Harry should be home by suppertime." She groaned and wondered if she could hide again all day. Her headache had cleared, but, like the coward she felt herself to be, she cringed at the thought of exposing herself to anyone.

"I can't face him, she said aloud. "That blonde bimbo will have convinced him I am an 'oar' after he has seen the newscast. How can I explain this to him. He'll probably cancel our contract—all because I saved a young boy from drowning. And all because I didn't get dressed but started baking doughnuts. "It shouldn't have mattered. There was no one here but us gals."

Laurie slowly sat up and made ready to have a hot soak in the bathtub. "I need to loosen any tense muscles. Don't I?" she murmured to herself as she climbed into the tub.

A knock on the door saw Sukie and Armand peeking in. Armand pushed and tried to climb into the tub with Laurie.

"Gram sent me up to see if you were ready for breakfast. She heard the water running." Sukie paused and looked her over. "You were sort of green looking yesterday."

"Thanks a load, kid. You'd better take your half of Armand out of here and go tell my mom I will be down in half an hour."

Having got out of the bath, she couldn't decide what to wear. Rummaging through her chifforobe, she looked over the new selection of dresses Harry had bought her. I need a diversion, if he is as angry as I expect, she thought. This green with the heart-shaped neckline should do the trick. After all, one has to don armor when going into battle.

"Oh, Harry, how could I know that the cameramen would take such pictures and then show them on television? The pictures were bad enough in the newspaper. I can't hide, so I might as well follow my Girl Scout oath to be prepared," she told herself. With that resolution firm in her mind, she marched downstairs.

As soon as she finished her breakfast of bacon, corn bread covered with gravy and two cups of coffee Laurie asked, "Are we ready for church this morning?"

Maybelle answered, "You know I always go. I'll be taking Suzanne with me, but you'd better not show your face there. One look at your dress and they will believe any gossip that's going around. Also, a few reporters are still out there at the gate."

To Laurie's chagrin, a tear trickled down her cheek, and then another. She mopped up with her napkin. Maybelle came and gave her a pat on her shoulder and a gentle squeeze.

"This will pass, you know. Once you have seen Harry, he will straighten everything out." She gave her another pat. "He's a good man." Reaching out to Sukie, she said, "Come, let's go."

"I don't want to go. I want to be here with Mom. She needs me if Daddy is angry at her. It was all my fault!" she cried out as she tried to cling to her.

"Your father isn't expected until late afternoon. You have plenty of time to go to church with Mother. You will see some of your schoolfriends and afterwards we can go see the Harringtons."

"I want to stay here with you," she begged, then defied her by saying, "Dad and I never go to church."

Maybelle took her hand. "Now is as good a time as any to find out what it's all about."

With a little nudging she was persuaded. "All right...OK, I'll go."

Maybelle dragged her out. The two set out to walk to the steepled white church down the road, past the Harringtons' place.

Laurie sat and brooded a while, then washed the

dishes. The roast was already in the oven and the timer was set for two o'clock. As she put away the dishes, she hummed part of "Amazing Grace", feeling more in the spirit of Sunday, then the vegetables were all washed and ready for cooking.

She thought, Why do I always get into such messy problems? I'm scared and Harry is so formidable. She wiped her eyes. I'm stupid! Being afraid won't get me very far, she thought. But—he's so big, he overpowers me at times. Well, he didn't overpower me in bed. I was ready, willing and able. We were one together; his gentleness and sweetness were what made it a magic time beyond all expectation.

She closed her eyes to cherish the feeling of closeness and beauty that had been established between them. I'd better stop dreaming and clean out our room. At least, I think it is still our room. Mother and Sukie will be back before I know it. She sighed.

The bedroom was a restful room. Her dad, just before he died, had had it done over especially for her in her favorite colors of Irish green and ivory, with sham pillows with petit point in a brilliant-colored floral pattern... Mother hasn't touched her needlework since I came home, Laura realized. I should try to get her started again. Maybe something special for Sukie...

After making her bed with fresh sheets, blanket and bedspread she admired the way the ivory scalloped edges set off her Irish green cover. Quickly she dusted her large mahogany chest of drawers and dressing table, then put everything back in place, her fingers caressing Harry's dish where he collected all his change, and his brush and comb.

She drew back the curtains and opened the door, stepping out onto the small balcony. It looked out at the orchards in back of the house. The apples and peaches scented the air; they were ready to pick now. She loved this view. With a sigh, she went back in, drawing the curtains again. She went into the bathroom and watered her spider plant hanging in front of the window. The room reflected the same colors as her bedroom. A tranquil room.

When she was midway down the stairs, the front door crashed open. An angry Harry dropped his luggage and advanced to the foot of the stairs as he stripped off his jacket and tie, dropping them right and left. His eyes bored into hers. His face looked as if it was cased in granite.

"Why were my calls here not answered?" The unforgiving look on his face caused Laurie to stand paralyzed with her hand gripping the rail in a life-threatening hold. Her mouth was open as she had started to scream at his invasion. Now it dropped even further. She gasped as she tried to breathe, letting out her breath in one large whoosh. "Oh-h-h!" Her chest hurt.

"No words of 'Hi! Glad to see you! Welcome home Harry'?" He looked around. "Where are Sukie and Maybelle? Is she soaked to the gills as usual?"

Sinking down onto the stair, she whispered back, "They went to church and should be here shortly." She'd been left spineless and hurt from the nasty crack about Maybelle. It might be true, but she wasn't always that way.

"Just as well. Let's get upstairs where we can be in private before they arrive. We need to talk." He looked her up and down with acute dislike.

Laurie sat there, all eyes and turning whiter if possible. She started to rise, but halfway up she collapsed, the room spun into outer space, and she started leaning forward in a faint. Harry caught her before she tumbled down the stairs. He heaved her into his arms and carried her up to bed. He stood looking at her with the fury oozing out of him. She looked so defenseless.

He turned, locked the door and went to get a cold,

wet facecloth. As he applied it to her forehead, her eyes fluttered open.

A half-hour later the door crashed open again. "Hi, Mom, I'm home!" Sukie yelled out. "I'm hungry. Isn't dinner ready?"

Maybelle, following in her path, stooped to pick up the jacket and tie. "Sukie, I think he's here already."

"Who's he?" she turned to query.

"Your father. Who else would leave a trail of clothes on the floor? What other man could be here?"

"My father always hangs his clothes; he never leaves them on the floor. That fink Hans Depner is the kind that would do so—Daddy said. And he would love to get his hands on her if he knew that Daddy wasn't here."

"That's no way to talk of a fine gentleman like Mr. Depner. He is to be the next new county registrar, I'll have you know."

Sukie started for the stairs. Maybelle grabbed her and yelled, "This is your father's coat. Keep away from them. They are newly wed and need some privacy."

"Not if he's angry at her. It wasn't her fault that those reporters took pictures of her."

"You don't hear any shouting, do you, or noise? So they are not fighting. Leave them in peace."

"I don't know, Grandma. True, that doesn't sound like Daddy. He likes to raise the roof when he isn't happy."

"How do you know that he isn't happy? They might have kissed and made up."

"If you say so, Grandma." Sukie looked up the stairs, upset but not knowing what to do about it. She retreated to the kitchen and quietly helped set the Wedgwood Sunday dinner dishes and Maybelle's sterling silverware on the ivory-colored tablecloth with drawn-stitch embroidery.

Then she sneaked to check the stairs—"Just in case

they show up''—but all she heard or saw was a mumble of voices—no yelling.

Maybelle found a half-bottle of wine. At two o'clock, they sat down to eat, not waiting any further for the couple. A couple of glasses helped down what dinner she was able to eat. Sukie had lost her appetite. Slowly, Maybelle hand-washed the dishes and silver while Sukie dried.

"I'm going for a nap, child." Seeing the worried frown on her face, she told Sukie, "Don't worry; he will come out when he is good and ready." Grabbing the remains of her bottle, she then hung up the telephone receiver, which started to ring before she reached the foot of the stairs. "Don't answer it, Sukie. Let it ring. Go out and play if you can't stand the noise," she said as she climbed upstairs.

After the sixth ring, Harry picked up the phone and listened for five seconds, then slammed down the receiver. In another few seconds it rang again. He lifted it up and this time set it down easily and waited for the count of five and listened again. He dropped the receiver off its stand. "So this is why you didn't answer the phone calls I made?" he asked as he stood over her.

She nodded, refusing to look at him or defend herself or explain. So far he hadn't allowed her to do any of those things. He wasn't giving her time to think either so she dug her heels in and refused to respond to his acrimonious, bitter, caustic accusations. She sat on the edge of the bed, looking at the rug, hoping the floor would cave in.

In exasperation he shook his head. "At least tell me why you were prancing around almost nude with cameras on you. Were you planning on joining the girls in *Playboy* magazine?" There was a long silence before Laurie looked up with glazed eyes.

He gave up. "Oh, hell! I'm going to the hospital to get my notes ready for tomorrow."

Sukie heard his footsteps coming down, and met him at the foot of the stairs. "It wasn't Mom's fault she was photographed in her underwear. It was all my fault." She gulped some air. "You didn't beat her, did you?"

"Oh, for heaven's sake, I never touched her, and I never would—and you don't have to take the blame for her exposing herself in public!" he shouted as he slammed out of the house. Then his car spun gravel as he drove down the drive.

"Mom, he didn't beat you, did he?" Sukie asked, walking into the bedroom.

"No, Sukie, your father isn't one to hit women or children. He never hit you, did he?"

"Not that I can remember. My mother spanked me a lot." She laid her head on Laurie's shoulder as she sat beside her. "I tried to tell him how it happened, but he didn't listen. It was my fault," she cried out.

"I know, sweet. Men do at times go off half-cocked with a set-in-stone idea and we have to allow them time to cool off. Time when they can stop and think," Laurie said, hugging her daughter and pushing her hair back off her face. "Hush now, hush, dear; we all need time to think a bit. Before you know it, he'll decide to listen to our side of the story.

"In the meantime, Sukie, you can ask Maybelle to call and ask Delia if she could come and make a light supper for us all. As this is her day off, she is to do nothing fancy. Now I have my splitting headache again. Could you bring me a cup of tea and I will find some aspirin in the bathroom? I think I'll go back to bed."

Harry gave up on his notes in disgust, reached into his desk's bottom drawer, brought out a bottle of Scotch, poured himself two fingers, and downed it in one swallow.

A head peeked around his door. "What's keeping you here so late when you have a new bride at home?"

"Oh, come in, Crinden." He stood and waved him to the only other chair in the room besides his. "Sit down for a moment. Can I offer a Scotch? Plain or with water?"

"Not right now, thanks; I still have to drive home and to catch up on my sleep cuddled up to Erma. You'd better go home and do the same or you will have a rough time tomorrow. Oh, I forgot; it's two a.m. now." He peered at Harry over his glasses. "Does your drinking have anything to do with Dr. Proctor's resignation?"

"Probably." He looked abashed and embarrassed.

"None of my business, but does it have anything to do with Friday evening's news? When Laurie saved the life of Sean Harrington?"

Harry sat straight up in his chair. "Saved whose life? I didn't see any saving of a life." More like the death of a million pop-eyed men, he thought darkly.

"I can imagine all you saw was her enticing figure in her bikini."

"Bikini!" he shouted. "She was in her underwear, for God's sake. That bra left nothing to the imagination." He ran his hand through his hair, standing it up on end.

"Don't let it get to you. You have seen worse on television and you know it. Saving a life was more important than modesty."

"But that was my wife. I don't want her to become a sideshow. Those photographers definitively had raunchy ideas in their pants. If there was any rescue. I didn't see it."

"Naturally. You didn't notice Laurie performing CPR on the boy she dragged out of the pool," Dr. Crinden said, with a twinkle in his eyes. "Did you see Suzanne at all? She was talking to the Harringtons as the boys were placed into the ambulance."

"I can't say I did." Harry collapsed in his chair. "I

was too busy trying to protect my wife's reputation from Ann's snide remarks.''

"Some women don't know when to let go. It's just as well she is leaving the area as of today. Fortunately, I know a young doctor who would like to join us.''

They both sat quietly to think their own thoughts. Then Dr. Crinden got up and stretched a bit. "I need to get to bed. If there is no emergency, I won't be in until noon.''

"Thanks a lot. I have a lot to think over, but I'd better leave this mess—'' he indicated his notes, which were strewn all over the desk "—and get home.''

"About time. Goodnight.'' Crinden waved his hand and went noisily down the hall.

Harry spilled his papers together and shoved them into the desk drawer, turned off the light and locked the door behind him.

He took his time driving with his window open a crack, hoping the air would clear his mind and get some of the fumes from his drink out of his system. One drunk in the family was enough.

I guess I didn't see what I should have, he thought. I was too busy listening to Ann's gloating. I didn't realize she had such a caustic tongue until I turned on her. She knew our affair was short and finished a long time ago. She's a good doctor in her field. That's why I recommended her when she applied for the job. I never knew she had such a foul mouth. It was an eye-opening experience.

Harry was beginning to wonder if he'd been wrong. Why didn't she answer and tell me how this all came about? he asked himself. Did I give her time to answer? She has always been quick enough to answer back at any other time. I probably didn't... He could feel the anger rising up again. I was too upset at her exposing herself to the cameras, showing on television that which is for my personal enjoyment only.

On entering the house, he took off his shoes and climbed swiftly to their bedroom door. Taking care not to let the door squeak, he opened it quietly. He crept up to the bed and watched her restless sleep. She murmured to herself.

He turned and went to the bathroom, took a quick shower and hurried back to the bed. Lifting the bedlinen and blankets carefully, he dropped his damp towel and climbed in, rolling over carefully toward Laurie. He caressed and pushed back some of her hair, only to find her pillow was damp with tears. He snuggled up to her, smoothing her hair. She turned into his arms. Not once waking.

The effort to control his libido was hard to maintain. It took its toll of him. Eventually he fell asleep, until his daughter woke him up, wanting to cuddle up with her mom to keep warm. When she found her dad in bed, she didn't know what to do.

Harry heard her and signaled for her to go on the other side while he got out of the bed and wrapped the damp, cold towel around himself.

He gasped as goosebumps crawled up his body. He hopped as fast as he could toward the bathroom and hot water. "Brrr." Laurie heard his groan and opened one eye to see what was happening just as the shock of cold feet hit her legs.

"What in the world…?" She lifted her head to see who had attacked her.

Sukie blinked at her. "I had to warm my feet, didn't I?"

"Yes, but not on me," was the whispered answer. "Who's in the shower?" she asked.

"Dad," was the sleepy response.

Harry dressed in record time and shaved in a cloud of steam. He returned to look at his wife and daughter, both already back asleep. Leaning over, he gave each a swift kiss and departed. Would she talk to him tonight? he wondered.

CHAPTER EIGHT

AFTER a run of mild Indian summer days, the weather had turned and brought in a rainy, gloomy, cold, raw day which seemed to go hand in hand with everyone's attitude in the house—that being *crabby*. It was a good thing Harry had had the roof repaired, so the water wasn't leaking in as usual.

He's done a lot of good for us and now we've made the whole family cross, Laurie acknowledged. Well, he didn't have to yell at me and accuse me of being deliberately provocative for the press and video cameras. I didn't even know they were there—much less pose for them.

Laurie sat down on the cushioned kitchen chair and clasped her head. She had a headache and couldn't see a way out of her dilemma. She wasn't about to put up with that type of attitude...but why was he sleeping in bed with her? He hadn't touched her and there were certainly enough rooms to sleep in other than hers. He hadn't canceled their contract, which should have told her something. Couldn't he just ask her to explain what happened without yelling at her?

I just don't understand men! she thought. It's true that I am just as much at fault for punishing Maybelle and Sukie by not speaking to Harry. I guess I should try and lighten up a bit around them, but when we are alone that's a horse of a different color. He's not going to treat me like Ralph did...

Oh, heck, he is a finer man than Ralph ever was, she

told herself. Why are you trying to compare them? You just don't like to be yelled at. Stop feeling sorry for yourself and grow up. You're an actress and when in company you can project a happier attitude. Get yourself up and make breakfast and try to smile a bit.

Laurie had dressed in warm trousers and a loose green sweater and had coffee and hot oatmeal ready for breakfast when Harry, neat in a business suit, and Sukie, in her school clothes, came downstairs.

"Good morning, Laurie."

"Good morning, Mom."

Both sat down as they greeted her.

Laurie gave a nod to her husband and gave Sukie a pat on the head, placing a hot cup of cocoa in front of her, and went around the table to fill Harry's and her cup with coffee. Not saying a word or looking at Harry, she filled their bowls with hot cereal and served them.

"Ugh, must I eat this?" Sukie scowled as she added brown sugar and milk in the bowl and started to mix it up.

"I'm afraid so," her father said as he dug into his bowl. "It will warm you up on a day like this." But he looked rather questionably at his dish as he hurriedly swallowed a sip of coffee to wash it down. If his daughter hadn't been watching him so closely, he'd have found some excuse to dump it in the garbage.

"Just what we need to get our corpuscles moving." He glanced over at Laurie.

Her face was without color, her eyes dull with a blank stare. Her movements were on automatic drive. As he looked, Harry had a twinge of conscience. But why shouldn't I get angry because she won't answer my questions? he asked himself. Wiping his mouth, he kissed Sukie and stormed out of the house.

"I wish you and Dad would talk to each other. I reckon—" Laurie smiled as this was a new expression for Sukie "—I don't know which is worse to hear—my mother and dad yelling at each other or this total silence.'' She toyed with her cereal.

"I'm sorry, Sukie, if this bothers you, but even adults have their off days.'' She paused a moment as she stared inwardly. "Eat up, dear. You can stay home until I can talk to your principal. I'll call in your excuse and make an appointment to see her. I've work to do at the hospital today. While I am gone, you need to make your bed and clean up your room. Delia will be here around ten o'clock, and she'll give you and Mother lunch. I don't want you to go out of the house except to air Armand. Do we understand each other?''

"Yeah. Can I watch television?''

"I would rather you didn't watch any of the daytime programs. We've got plenty of videos you can pick from. Your dad supplied you with a good selection.'' Harry had brought a TV set and a VCR with him to the house. "How about reading the book you need to read for homework?''

"OK, if I have to,'' she agreed as she scraped up the last of her oatmeal and placed her dishes in the washer.

Feeling depressed, Laurie managed to get herself ready for work, wearing a conservative jade two-piece suit. No make-up now, as she had already used it heavily for her enactment... Now, why did Harry still sleep in their bed if he was so upset about the TV pictures of her working on Sean semi-nude? she wondered again. She certainly hadn't done it on purpose.

At work, Laurie found she was slated to project a case of diabetic peripheral neuropathy. She got dressed for her performance. Never having had such a disease, she hoped she could be convincing. The fact that she was conscious that the interns might have seen the broadcast made her stomach curdle. Well, she'd always prided herself on her acting ability. She closed her mind to all else and went to perform.

She entered the classroom pulling herself along with a cane. Walking on one foot and placing the right one down carefully, she whined and grimaced. "Oh, the pain is excruciating!" she howled. Felder dashed to the front to place a chair under her.

Her leg was extended as the foot and knee were swollen. She had dipped them in several layers of wax and rubbed them with liniment. It also helped keep the premeds at a distance. The smell was a bit sharp.

"How did this start?" a student asked.

"Suddenly," she replied.

"Are you taking special medicines for anything?"

"Just Percocet for pain, Glucotrol for borderline diabetes, and Furosemide for blood pressure. Here's my list."

They took her blood pressure and required blood tests for her diabetes. They felt her legs, trying to find her foot pulse, and couldn't. After two hours of her beating on the desk behind her and yelling with pain, the class of puzzled pre-interns were finally released and so was Laurie.

"That was quite a performance. How did you get your legs and knees so swollen?" the instructor asked.

She told her. "I carry everything in my kit I need to change my appearance."

"And how do you expect to show sugar in your blood test?"

"Through syrup-doctored cola which I have been drinking, and the placebos were my Glucotrol tablets and blood-pressure pills."

"Oh, you sneaky thing; that's great. You sure have them buffaloed." They both laughed as they left the lecture hall.

"Hey, did you hear Dr. Proctor suddenly left us?" Nurse Hart stopped to tell Laurie as they passed in the hall.

"Did she give a reason?" Between her and Mrs.

Wilson, they'd been doing a fine job on herself and Sukie, she thought wryly.

"Only that she had a better offer in France. She really didn't fit in here."

"I'm glad that she left."

An hour later, after lunchtime, she was on her way to talk to the school principal, Mrs. Whitmore. She knocked on the door marked "Principal's Office". "Come in," a voice called out. The salt-and-pepper-haired, congenial-looking woman stood up to greet her.

"Mrs. Mason, I believe."

"Yes, I'm Laurie Mason. Suzanne's stepmother."

"Please, sit down. I am so glad to meet you. Suzanne has praised you every time we have talked. The Harringtons called to say how courageous you and Suzanne were in saving Neil and Sean's lives."

Before Laurie could open her mouth, Mrs. Whitmore continued, "Mr. Mason spoke to me about some of the problems arising from the fight and name-calling Suzanne had last week. *I* was not told what was actually said that started the fight. Mr. Mason repeated it to me. Also, Mrs. Wilson's treatment of the Cherokee label placed on you.

"I can only apologize for not digging deeper at the time. Mrs. Wilson has been reprimanded and will be suspended until the school board meets to decide if she should be fired. She has been with us for several years and is in desperate need of work, but we cannot allow such negligence, let alone compounding it with gossip detrimental to others."

She'd left Laurie with nothing to say. She had worked up a full head of steam to roll over Mrs. Wilson and Mrs. Whitmore. Now she could only nod in agreement and slowly deflate. So Harry had been busy this morning. It seemed both her problems were taken care of, leaving her only with the problem of what to do about Harry.

On the way home, she swore never to speak to him until he cooled down and allowed her to explain what had happened without yelling at her. After Ralph, she'd vowed never to be dominated by any male. Her stomach churned and, having been deprived of a good out-and-out fight, she was at odds with herself. She didn't know whether to cry or to be relieved.

A week passed in which everyone but Sukie acted as if they were walking on a tightrope. Harry left right after breakfast and didn't show up until suppertime. He talked with Sukie and helped with her homework if she needed it. Later, he left to go back to the hospital if an emergency arose, or closed himself in the den that he'd turned into a workroom for himself, adding an Irish green carpet, a file cabinet, a bigger oak desk combined with a console for a computer and a typewriter, forming a semi-circle around his chair. With "in" and "out" baskets, he was able to catch up on some of his paperwork.

Harry still slept beside Laurie and she found her dreams were much improved, leaving an empty space. She nearly wept for her loneliness of spirit and heart.

The antique mahogany desk from the den went into a small morning room. Maybelle was thrilled and started to use it, writing to old friends, Sadi Lloyd and Corabell Johnson, and planning to see them.

Sukie was much happier at school with a new, younger teacher, Miss Clemons. Neil Harrington became her defender and protector and dogged her footsteps. Twice she brought her new friends, Lou Ellen and Polina, home after school to play and they helped Laurie mix batches of cookies to bake and eat. Also, to clean up the mess afterwards. It did Laurie's heart good to hear the trilling voices of happy girls. They were invited to a slumber party for the following Friday.

Maybelle stopped her wine-drinking except for a glass at suppertime. She started to attend some social functions at the country club. Harry gave her a modest allowance, which boosted her confidence. She had a few old friends in for tea, and she was blossoming out and using taxis to get herself around. A former admirer, Mr. Emmett Royce, a widower, looking for a companion, latched onto her, much to her delight.

Everyone seemed brighter and happier except Laurie. She felt she was disconnected from herself. She continued as the hospital's standardized patient, leaving a little too much time to think and brew.

She was trying to read a new novel in the living room one afternoon, when Sukie arrived home from school.

"Mom, I'm home." The back door crashed open and shut.

"So I hear, dear. How did your day go?"

"Oh, all right." She passed it off as being insignificant. "You know, the high school is having a play about the folks that came over the mountains from Virginia, North and South Carolina—and I forgot the name of the other place," she went on, nonstop. "Can we go to it? They asked me to try and sell some tickets." Sukie had bounced into the living room and dropped her backpack and patchwork quilted jacket in a chair. She dropped an envelope into her lap.

"I'm glad you had a good day. Did you get all your homework handed in?"

"Yeah, Miss Clemons smiled at me and said to keep up the good work. Well! Open the letter." She was quivering with excitement. "Can we go? It will be on a Friday night so there will be no school the next day. We can stay up late." She hung onto the arm of Laurie's chair, hopping up and down.

Laurie opened the envelope. "This note says the play will be in three weeks on the Friday and Saturday and some of the mothers are making cookies and punch for everyone. Can I help?'' After reading the dates and times on the tickets, she commented, ''That should be fun. Let's see what your father thinks about it. I will buy tickets for us all and hope that he can make it. You can ask him tonight. I think Maybelle would enjoy it and she may talk Mr. Royce into accompanying her. I saw a similar play on the same subject when I was in grammar school.''

''Oh, goody! If I sell fifty tickets, I can get in free—won't that be great?'' she said as she kicked her shoes off.

''You can come with me now to the hospital—now is the best time to find a crowd, before others beat you to the punch—and then we can see how much of a salesperson you can be... Get your drink and cookie while I get ready.''

For once, as they entered the hospital it seemed rather quiet. They made their way to Harry's office.

''Come in,'' a voice rang out as they knocked. ''Ah, Mrs. Mason and Miss Mason. How nice to see you.'' Mary Beth Thomas, Harry's secretary, greeted them. ''Harry will be down from the OR in a short time, I believe. I take it you want to see him?''

''I've come to sell him some tickets to the play about the first men and settlers that came here over the Appalachian Mountains. Would you like to buy some?'' Sukie held out some tickets. ''It will be in three weeks on a Friday and Saturday night at the high school. They are five dollars a ticket for adults and two dollars fifty for children and students.''

''Oh, thank you, Sukie. I would love to take two. I acted in a similar play when I was in high school. Would you like to wait here for Dr. Mason? Or—'' she looked questioningly at them ''—a good place to sell tickets while you are waiting is in the cafeteria. It's time for a change of shift and coffee break. There should be someone there.''

''Thank you, Mary Beth, we'll do just that.''

Sukie made the rounds of the tables with her tickets, talking up a storm, while Laurie had a cup of tea and a slice of blackberry pie. She was amazed how Sukie had expanded from a sulky girl to this vibrant child. Several of the premed doctors came to chat with Laurie for a few minutes. Felder expounded on some of their diagnoses, and she nodded and acted as if she knew something about it. As she was getting ready to yawn, he stopped in mid-stream.

''Dr. Mason.'' Felder blushed and excused himself. ''I'll see you, Laurie.'' And he hurried away.

Laurie blinked at the sudden quiet surrounding her. Everyone seemed to have stopped talking. She swallowed and gulped and met Harry's dark, contemptuous eyes. Now what have I done? I'm here in a public room having a boring conversation. Certainly that's not anything to get upset over. Her bewildered look changed quickly to hide her feelings.

Harry noted how her soft hazel eyes changed from questioning to nothing.

''Mary Beth said you and Sukie were down here selling tickets,'' he said as he sat down opposite her.

''Daddy!'' A whirlwind struck him and arms around his neck nearly strangled him. ''I sold ten tickets, plus the four you are going to buy.''

''Whoa there, let me breathe.'' He pried her off and swung her up in his arms. ''What's this about you selling tickets?''

''I can get in for free if I sell fifty tickets.''

''You'd better let me see the ticket so I can see if it's worth wasting my money,'' Harry teased.

''Dad, you've got to buy four tickets. Mom, Maybelle and I want to go even if you can't go. Maybelle said she will see that Mr. Royce buys one also.'' She pleaded,

"Please, Dad...here are the tickets." She counted them out into his hand.

"Ah. A play based on the over-mountain men crossing through the mountain gaps to settle in what was the Cherokee Indian lands. That sounds as if it might be interesting and teach us a bit about this mountain range and how the settlers made the crawl up and down the ridges." He looked up and asked his wife, "Are you interested in going?" She gave a nod of her head. "How much did you say you were scalping me?" he asked Sukie.

"Daddy, stop teasing." She started counting with her fingers. "Five, ten, fifteen for three of you," she said as she pressed one finger then another. "Sixteen, seventeen dollars and fifty cents for all of us."

Harry dug his wallet out. "It looks like I have nothing smaller than a twenty-dollar bill." He held the bill in his hand. "Do I get my money back if you sell enough tickets?"

"Oh, Dad, you are a tease."

"Got any change?"

"I think so; let me look." She dumped out her pocketbook and looked at her change. She wrote down twenty dollars on a piece of paper, subtracting seventeen dollars and fifty cents. Chewing her pencil in her mouth, she looked down and started working out the difference. Her fingers got to work again and then she exclaimed, "Two dollars and fifty cents!" Then she sorted out the bills and passed the right amount to her father.

"Looks as if you could be a pretty good salesperson," he said, placing his change in his wallet. "Are we ready to leave?" he asked. "I thought it would be nice for all of us to have dinner out. There is a new Italian restaurant just opened up. Everyone praises it."

Laurie looked at Sukie. "How about you? Do you think you would like real Italian spaghetti?"

"Couldn't I have just plain hamburgers? I like the

spaghetti you make because you leave out the yucky stuff like garlic and onions, and only put in a little of that flaky junk oregano.''

"I suspect we could arrange a hamburger for you. But you may be missing something special if you don't try it out.''

"Oh, yeah! No way, José! I don't want to ruin my insides.''

"Well, let's get going and we can stop and see if Maybelle will join us. I've already told Delia not to fix dinner. Is that all right with you, Laurie?''

She nodded. He could have asked me sooner instead of springing it on me at the last moment, she thought.

She drove herself home as Sukie decided to go with her father. What's the matter with me? she asked herself. I feel guilty, when I have nothing to be guilty about. I miss him, but I will not let him treat me as Ralph did. He could at least say he's sorry for yelling at me or say he loves me...

Do I really love him or is this just—infatuation? The sex was so wonderful that I miss it. Now that I have had a taste of that pleasure, just thinking about that night makes all of my groin muscles tighten up. I don't really know if I am coming or going. What a pathetic specimen I am, and I can't cry on his shoulder. At the rate we're going we'll be lucky if we get to the end of our ninety days—

Stop feeling so sorry for yourself and put some iron in your spine. Remember you are an actress. Try to sound happy and carefree instead of ruining everyone's happiness.

Harry stopped at his office to pick up some papers he needed to take home and work on.

"Hey, Dad, I told Mom I would go home with you. Is that all right?'' Sukie barged into his office.

"You bet." He slid his papers into his briefcase. "Let's go."

"Dad, why are you mad with Mom, and why doesn't she speak to you?" Not waiting for an answer, she went on, "It wasn't her fault that Neil and Sean were in the pool. I got the key and opened the gate when Neil called me a bad name. Mom had already told me not to open the gate or let anyone inside unless you or she were with me." Her tears started to trickle down. Harry sat down, took out a white handkerchief, swung her into his lap and let her dry her tears.

"You and my mother used to yell all the time but what did you do that Mom won't talk to you?"

"It's hard to explain how grown-ups react to problems. The same way as you can't explain why you allowed Neil to talk you into opening the pool gate. I only listened to gossip and got the wrong idea. I was so shocked at the pictures on the television that I really didn't see anything but Laurie half-nude... When I got home, I had worked up a big head of steam and let it out full blast."

"Oh, Daddy, that wasn't very clever." She shook her head.

"I know it now, but at the time I couldn't see straight. The same as you didn't see straight in allowing Neil to talk you into something you knew you shouldn't do. I'm not sure why she won't forgive me, so I will have to work on it."

"Mom forgave me when I confessed how wrong I was in using the key, and the Harringtons accepted my 'I'm sorry' and Neil and I both promised not to do it again... Did you tell Mom how sorry you were for yelling at her?" Sukie looked up to find her father's eyes were looking everywhere but at her. He squirmed and then lifted her off his lap.

"Let's get home and take Mom out for the evening."

It turned out to be a struggle for Harry to keep a conversation going that evening. Sukie enjoyed her hamburger and French fries, but turned her nose up at grits. She sampled some of Laurie's spaghetti. "Ugh!"

Laurie laughed. "Wait until you grow up; things will taste different."

After eating, Sukie managed to sell two more tickets as she bragged about the play and how Laurie's father's ancestors were among the original settlers at that time and Maybelle's family came from Atlanta, Georgia.

"We'll have to, some time, take a run up to Jonesboro, the oldest town in Tennessee," Laurie recommended.

Harry reached over for the coffee pot, pouring some more in each cup to warm it up. "You know, one of the premeds was telling me about a trip one can make in the fall. Too late for this year. Some of the premeds plan to walk it the same way the over-the-mountain men did it originally. There is a highway now, so you can walk the trail or drive up the road. You can start at Linville, North Carolina through the Roan Mountain Gap.

Take Route Nineteen West to the town of Elizabethton in Tennessee.

"We could take a picnic with us and walk part of the way or drive the full length. There are mountain laurels, azaleas, and the thick forests of rhododendrons along the Unaka Ridges are a glory to see in the spring, or early September, I'm told."

"Awesome! Can Neil, Sean and maybe Todd go with us? A picnic would be so stupendous! Can we, Dad, can we?" Sukie hopped up and down.

Laurie spoke up. "Let's not plan too far ahead. In the meantime we can see places closer to home. When we get home, we can ask Maybelle which are the best places. She might want to go with us. She took me when I was your age, but it's been quite a while since I have been to some of those places. I will need to get out some road maps. Let's see what we can do next weekend."

Harry looked at Laurie. "If Sukie is having a slumber party, we can take the girls too for the day. How does that sound to you? I have the weekend off."

"Great! Matter of fact, I think I can remember just the place to start—a log cabin; the site is called Rocky Mount. It dates back to the late 1700s and everything is authentic. If I can figure out how to get there."

Friday after school, Sukie, Polina and Lou Ellen did their homework after a lot of persuasion and bribing with a promise of baking cookies as soon as homework and dinner were finished. Delia was getting ready a supper of fried catfish, spoonbread and baked kidney bean casserole. Lou Ellen and Polina said it was one of their favorite dinners other than hamburgers. Sukie looked very dubious. "Ugh, must I...?" she asked.

"Well, unless you try it, you will never know if you like it, Laurie told her."

"Catfish doesn't sound very good. I saw a picture of one and it looked horrid, with whiskers all over its face."

"You know you like fish and chips. We have had it several times. Actually, I make it using fillet of catfish and you've never noticed the difference."

"Ugh! Really? It sounds gruesome. Why didn't you tell me?" Her face was all screwed up, showing her objections.

"Well, if you don't learn to eat the things we eat here in the south, you will soon find your friends' mothers think you are too hoity-toity for them and won't ask you to eat with them again."

Sukie's nose elevated and she tried looking down it and they all broke out laughing.

"Well, I refuse to like grits and okra. I don't care what anyone thinks."

Laurie laughed. "Well, I confess that I'm not partial to them either."

About eleven-thirty, Harry went down to quiet the slumber party and convince them it was time to close their eyes. They were in their sleeping bags having sodas and cookies while they thoroughly scared themselves with horror stories.

"If you want to go exploring tomorrow, you do have to get some sleep."

"We do," the trio called out.

"OK, let me turn off the lights and anyone needing the downstairs washroom go now. I will leave the washroom light on so you can find your way to it if you need to go during the night."

"Oh, Dad, we know where it is."

Harry sat in the kitchen with a book to read while the whispering quieted down. At midnight, they were all asleep, and he gazed in at them, wondering if he and Laurie would have a child... "Why would I want a child with such an indiscriminate actress?" He spoke softly to himself. "What's the matter with me? She's not anything like Rebecca. Now she was indiscriminate... promiscuous even."

The sound of humming bees woke Laurie early. The sun was not really up and she wondered why bees would be in the house. Turning over, she opened one eye, looking around for the bees. The hum seemed to be coming from the door. Two pairs of blue eyes and one pair of brown were watching and the musical sound of bees humming came from the watching eyes.

"What are you girls doing up so early?" She spoke in a soft voice so as not to wake Harry. "Go downstairs and wait for me to get up. Sukie, pour each of you a glass of orange juice. I will be down shortly." Covering a yawn, she turned over and hugged her pillow. "Oh, God, why couldn't they sleep longer?"

After a few moments, she rolled carefully out of bed, grabbing a navy blue velour housecoat, and started downstairs.

"Coffee is what I need first," she muttered as she fumbled around the kitchen looking for the ingredients. The girls clustered around as she made her coffee, chatting away. "Girls, why don't you watch the Saturday morning cartoons while I wake up and then I will get your breakfast?"

"OK," chirped three voices.

"We decided we wanted waffles with loads of butter and honey and some maple syrup," Sukie said.

"OK, OK, I'll call you when I'm ready." And she collapsed, hugging her mug of coffee to warm her hands. After the second mug, she had wakened enough to look around for her breakfast makings. Not being the greatest cook, she tended to go for the easy option, and toasted frozen waffles were one of Sukie's favorites. Thank heavens Harry brought an oven toaster with him, she thought.

"Come, girls, it's all ready," she called a few minutes later. "You can take it into the living room. Hot chocolate coming up." Each had a small tray holding her warmed filled plate and mug. She carried through the gooey ingredients, and a pitcher of hot chocolate.

Harry strolled in, showered, dressed informally, and looking too handsome for her heart rate and blood pressure. "Good morning, Laurie," he said.

She nodded in reply as she squirmed in her chair, feeling righteous and guilty all at the same time. But no one makes a cipher out of me, she vowed silently. Not again.

"What can I make for your breakfast, Harry?"

"I see the girls are having a good time eating waffles, so if it isn't too much trouble, could I have four of your waffles with scrambled eggs and some of your home-made sausages? I think I can leave off the syrup and gooey the girls are enjoying.''

''Coming right up. Would you like a glass of orange juice while you wait?''

''Thanks for the offer, but coffee with the meal will be enough. As soon as we're finished here, we'll start on our voyage. Hop to it, girls. Clean up and brush your teeth before I do inspections.''

CHAPTER NINE

AFTER herding the girls to pick up after themselves and roll up their bedrolls, they were declared ready to leave.

Harry drove the blue and brown station wagon that he had gotten Laurie to replace her old wreck. He had shuddered every time he'd seen her drive it and his excuse for buying the new vehicle had been that it was in consideration of Sukie's safety.

The route to the log cabin wasn't far, if you were a crow flying there. The winding dirt and gravel and sometimes paved roads were scenic; they passed through the last of the fall colors, leaves dropping everywhere, and saw peaceful farms and cemeteries that were quiet and serene. On arriving at the Rocky Mount historical site, and parking in a lot across the road, they made their way to the wooden front door.

It opened before they knocked. "Howdy, folks, I am Mistress Holmsby; I don't see the stagecoach. Are you staying all night?"

"Hello," the girls sang out in harmony.

"I am Harry Mason and this is my wife, Laurie, and daughter, Suzanne." He placed a hand on her head and then on each girl's as he said their names. "Polina and Lou Ellen, friends of the family. I believe the coachman will be in shortly."

"Let me show you through the house and allow you to wash your hands. It's a long, dirty trip over the ridges. Did you come from the Carolinas or Georgia?"

"Carolinas," Laurie responded.

The girls got a kick out of pouring water into the washbasin, using home-made soap and drying their hands on bleached flour sacking. They dumped the used water into a slop bucket.

The bedrooms were small and the bedsprings were woven with flax rope springs and feather-quilt mattresses and covers.

"This feather blanket is neat!" Polina exclaimed. "The quilting is beautiful with the wedding-ring pattern."

"Hey, look, there's a roll-out bed under here and a pot." Sukie looked at their guide. "Why is that pot there?"

Mistress Holmsby explained. "It's called a chamber pot with a cover. If you need to go to the toilet, we have an outhouse. In the winter time, it's too cold to go out there. This is used in its place."

"Yuck!" exclaimed Lou Ellen. "That's gross."

"We don't have running water into the house. It has to be hand-carried from the spring." Mistress Holmsby turned to shepherd them out through the room Governor Blount had used for a while, then down the steep narrow steps, through the dining room to the back door and down to the outside kitchen. This was to prevent the house from burning down if something caught fire.

The kitchen had a huge fireplace with things cooking in large hanging pots, and a long table and a couple of chairs. The fire kept the room almost a little too warm. Herbs and onions hung from the rafters. Everything smelled delicious. The aroma of bread baking stirred up their appetites. "That smells scrumptious," Laurie commented. A small cup of soup which smelled and tasted delicious to her was handed to each of them. Followed by a slice of fresh bread with blackberry jam.

Polina, the most courageous, took a sip. "Well, it tastes all right, I guess—but it's not Mom's chicken soup."

Harry laughed. "Drink up, girls; you can brag about the settlers' soup when we go to see the play about the over-mountain men."

"My army friends in Europe would be amazed!" Sukie exclaimed as she manfully drank all of the soup.

A small pig was being roasted on a spit with a long handle you turned by hand.

They strolled out back of the kitchen to a short path leading beside a delicious-smelling herb garden to a weaving cabin. There were piles of sheep's wool ready to be carded and then spun to yarn on the spinning wheel. Tubs were used for dying the yarn and there were racks where it could be dried in bad weather; otherwise the yarn was dyed and dried outside. The weaving was done on a large frame for linens and blankets and clothing, whilst other items were done on a smaller one.

The girls stood there in awe, taking everything in. They were fascinated at the range of natural colors. Moving on, they enjoyed seeing a mother pig with her piglets in a split-rail fence. "They look so cute and cuddly," said Sukie. The sheep were cropping the green lawn as well as the fields. They saved on mowing the lawn with a sickle.

When the girls started to get restless, Harry took them back through the house to thank their hostess. There was a box for donations for the tour. Afterwards, they went through the museum, but as the girls were not too interested they soon left.

Exhausted, but wound up, the girls livened up the trip home with singing. They managed to get ten miles before they quit. Then they started telling jokes, seeing who could tell the corniest one.

Polina won with, "Why did the duck cross the playground?"

Sukie said, "'Cos the other ducks were there."

Harry said, "They wanted to see if the chickens had

the day off.'' Which had the girls doubled up with laughter.

''Oh, well, I guess I'd better tell you,'' Polina said, as the others couldn't come up with anything. ''Why did the duck cross the playground?'' Polina giggled. ''To get to the other slide!''

Laurie knew where a hamburger and ice-cream stand was. They treated the girls to a late lunch.

After that, the quiet suddenly hit Laurie, and she looked round in the car to see what the girls were up to. She gave a sigh of relief. They were fast asleep. The rest of the drive was quiet, with both Harry and Laurie deep in their own thoughts. Harry was feeling slightly guilty but was determined he was right. Laurie was trying to figure out how to lighten up and still not give in. She felt very put upon.

Soon Harry dropped Polina and Lou Ellen off at their homes. Laurie carried in their backpacks and bedrolls. Harry carried the children. ''They acted as if they had a wonderful time but they didn't get much sleep last night,'' Harry told the parents, who understood the problem.

Back home, Harry carried Sukie up to her bed while Laurie unloaded the station wagon. Then she went to help undress her daughter, also to carry a mug of hot chocolate to her. When she arrived, Harry had already gotten her tucked in. With her eyes half-closed, seeing Laurie holding the mug, Sukie sat up and reached for the warm chocolate.

''Thanks, Mom,'' she said as she finished it and laid back down. ''Do I get a kiss goodnight?''

''Sure do.'' Laurie bent to kiss her forehead and smooth out her hair and sheets. ''Sleep tight, dearest.''

And she and Harry walked out of the daintily decorated room, with its sheer rainbow-colored curtains and matching bedspread. The cream-colored wallpaper was offset by ballerinas dancing in a border all around the walls, the rug was a darker, multicolored weave, and two paintings—reproductions of Degas' *Dancer Tying Her Slipper* and *Practice At The Bar (a small child)*—hung over the head of her bed. The room was especially done up for Sukie.

She sighed. "If only we could remain in that age of innocence."

As they walked into their bedroom, Harry placed his hand on her shoulder and turned her around to face him. He started to say something, but instead drew her close and held her loosely in an embrace.

They stood quietly for what seemed eons to Laurie. Her head was cushioned under his chin, absorbing his scent, and her arms, without her realizing it, went around his waist as she pressed in a little closer. Her feet slid over, matching his shoes toe-to-toe. She heard his breathing quicken, as hers did. It felt wonderful. She almost felt sheltered and loved.

Oh, God, I really love him.

The thought so startled her that she started backing away from him.

He tried to tighten his hold, but she struggled and looked at him in terror, turning frantically to get away. His heart plunged. Loosening his hold, he stepped back and thought, What have I and Ralph done to her? He looked bleakly at her, started to say something and turned. He left the room quietly, in a daze, found his den, sat in front of his desk and placed his head in his hands. Groping for thoughts to explain what had gone wrong.

I know what went wrong—I listened to that Ann Proctor, he told himself. He reached for a handkerchief and wiped his eyes and blew his nose. What kind of a fool am I? I have very little discrimination with women, he thought. Laurie is the best thing that's happened to Sukie and me. I've ruined everything with my jealousy and now I'm too stubborn to admit it. As the expression goes, I carried things pretty far down the pike this time. Now what can I do to patch up everything and ask for her forgiveness?

Upstairs, Laurie fell across the bed, sobbing her eyes out. Why me, God? she cried silently. He frightened me for a moment when he didn't release me. I felt that he was Ralph all over again. It was so beautiful and comfortable to be held in his arms and I ruined it. I didn't realize till then that I had truly fallen in love with him.

She burst into another flood of tears and writhed on her bed in pain and shame. He didn't mean to force me and his hold wasn't tight, she acknowledged. He would never force me like Ralph did. So why did I make such a big deal over it? Each night he sleeps beside me, but doesn't touch me. Why? There must be something I can do to make up and start talking to him. That witch Dr. Proctor took her revenge on us both. Maybe he doesn't love her, but did he have to listen to her malign me? He should know that I'm not the type of person to go prancing about in a semi-nude state.

She dried her sniffles and blew her nose. Guess I should've known that people's opinions of an actress aren't too great. The first time he saw me I was almost stripped by the premeds, and that must have made him think that was my style. It was probably my red hair and temper; they always seem to get me into trouble— She sat up. Why did he want to marry me if he thought I was a loose woman? She frowned, and felt very sorry for herself for a few moments as she wiped the tears that trickled slowly down her face. One would have thought I would have dried up by now. I don't want to drag Sukie into our quarrel now that she has settled down and seems to be happy. It's not right to upset children with grown-up affairs.

She wiped away the remaining tears and got out of bed, picking up her sheer light green nightgown and robe before going in for a quick shower and putting cold packs on her eyes. There was no point in dressing up because she planned to get in bed as soon as they finished their supper. Life goes on and I can't bury myself every time my feelings are hurt, she told herself. Plus, I'd better try a peace offering of the supper Delia must have left in the refrigerator. While she rubbed herself dry, it dawned on her that Maybelle hadn't made an appearance when they'd arrived back. She guessed she was with Emmett. This thought upset her a bit. For a few moments she felt hollow inside. Then she told herself, grow up, stupid, and admitted that she couldn't think of anything better for her mother.

When her father had been ill Maybelle had nursed him by herself. He'd had a bad heart attack and they'd kept him in the hospital for a short while, then sent him home for Maybelle to take care of him, with only Delia and the visiting nurse helping out. He'd gradually become disoriented and hard to cope with.

After Dad died, Mother had very little comfort from me, Laurie acknowledged now. I was tied up in Boston trying to cut myself off from Ralph and pick up my own pieces before transferring back home. I had too many problems then myself.

She stared bleakly at nothing for a moment. Perhaps that's part of why Mother started drinking, she thought. I guess I wasn't much of a daughter at that point.

A quick peek into her mother's room showed there was no one there, and her bed didn't look as if she had slept there. She went down to see what Delia had left them. Steaks, potato salad and a vegetable salad were ready in the large refrigerator, along with a pumpkin pie. All she needed to do was grill the steaks and heat the pie a bit. A fresh warm pie tasted so much better than a cold one, and with whipped cream on the top that should do the trick.

Her eyes were bleak as she decided she'd better check and see if Harry had also gone. The house was too quiet.

I'm afraid to go to his den in case he doesn't want to be disturbed, she thought. Oh, heck, I have to find out if he wants to eat, don't I?

She tapped on the door. There was no answer, but a ray of light was reflecting on the floor. Just as she put her hand on the doorknob, she heard him say, "Come in."

Harry raised his head and watched her enter. She shines in the glory of her femininity. I didn't realize she was so beautiful! he thought.

Laurie's eyes were huge with an expression he didn't understand. He had seen her look at Sukie the same way. He'd thought it was an expression of love. Or at least of liking.

"Would you like some supper? Delia left all the fixings and it can be ready in half an hour?"

"Yes— I'm not too hungry just now. Can I help out?" Standing up, he made ready to follow her.

"You can get drinks for us and help set the table." She wondered what he'd been doing all this time. His desk was already cleared so he couldn't have been working.

With Laurie sipping at her bourbon and branch water, and Harry at his Scotch and soda, they worked quietly together, and soon the steaks were grilled and the pumpkin pie warming in the oven.

"Where is Maybelle? Isn't she coming down?"

"As far as I know she isn't here; she's probably with friends or Emmett."

They talked pleasantly of the day's activities, and how well the girls got along with each other.

The meal over, Harry wiped his mouth and put his napkin down. "Laurie, I do want you to know how much I appreciate the happiness you have given Sukie. This is the first time I have seen her so self-assured and happy. You and Maybelle have done a lot for her. She isn't rebelling at the world anymore.''

"Wait until she hits her teens and then you may really learn about rebelling.'' Laurie laughed. "She's a child that's easy to do things for and to like. Now that I'm not a blonde bimbo,'' Laurie added, teasing him a bit. "She has made friends and everything is straightened out at school, which makes all the difference. I've enjoyed watching her sprout up and being so cheerful.''

After cleaning up the kitchen, Laurie started for the stairs. Harry placed a hand on her shoulder to stop her.

"Could you stay a while and talk with me? We've seldom had enough time to get to know each other.''

Laurie turned and looked him in the eye. The pleading look she saw there turned her heart over. This man sure knows which buttons to push, she thought.

"I'll be pleased to. Although I'm tired, I can stay for a short while.''

Harry took her hand and walked into the living room to the couch. When they sat down, out of sheer nervousness, Laurie blurted out, "Tell me about when you were growing up. Where did you live and what made you decide to become a doctor and then a surgeon?''

He chuckled a bit. "My folks were tied up in army life but I was born here. We were visiting friends and family. I came early. My parents were raised on a farm here and their parents didn't live too far apart. Most summers, I spent one half of my time with my Mason grandparents and the other half with my Sutcliffe grandparents. That way I got to know most of my relatives. Other than that, I was the usual army brat. I think I decided to be a fireman or lawyer, policeman or doctor. It varied from time to time.''

"What finally made you decide?''

"I guess it was in Italy when we almost smashed into a four-car accident at a crossroad. I was upset at the way the people there handled the victims and let some almost bleed to death. Until Dad and I hauled out our emergency kit and bandaged the worst of the flow. We strapped two children with broken arms and legs too. Eventually someone managed to call the police and a couple of ambulances showed up. Dad and I took the people who could walk in our car to the hospital.''

"That must have been a traumatic episode. I hope it didn't give you nightmares?''

"I guess it did a couple of times. We did hear from the doctor who handled the patients. We received a very lovely inscribed placard with a letter to Dad's commander, praising us for the foresight to have a Red Cross kit with us. Two patients had eventually died of head wounds, but the doctors and patients felt we had saved many lives. Everyone had signed the placard—even those who couldn't write had signed with an X.

"Dad's commander handed him his placard in a special ceremony, with his unit all in parade uniforms. And honor guards' flags were waving in the breeze, with the doctors and several of the people who were injured in attendance. I have the placard now, buried in some of the boxes up in the attic.''

"How lovely. No wonder you were so insistent on setting up the station wagon with emergency supplies in a waterproof container!''

"Well, that's why I decided to study medicine. I signed up to do my resident training in the service and Dr. Callum, a friend of the family, felt I had the hands for surgery. When I finished my tour, I then trained here, Stateside. I returned to the army after I graduated and served my time in Germany and Washington DC.''

"Well, that has certainly been a varied life.''

"Laurie, now it's your turn to tell me a little more about the time when you grew up here.'' He squeezed her hand gently and held it, then placed his other hand around her back. She was so eager to hear what he was saying, she didn't realize what he was doing.

"Well, I suspect I had a normal happy childhood. Dad was great on the history of sections of the Carolinas and here in the Appalachian Mountains of Eastern Tennessee. He took me and Maybelle all over the place. One year, when the Overmountain Victory National Historic Trail was being opened, Dad and I carried our bedrolls, dry clothes and some food and hiked from Elizabethton across the ridges and into the Carolinas. It took a long time to get there and back. We used all of Dad's vacation time, I remember. Now we can travel the trail in a few hours of driving time."

"My word! How old were you then?"

"I think about ten or eleven. We sure had a grand time. Some of the boys from school were making the trip too.

"After high school, I won a scholarship to a Boston school of acting. About the time I was getting noticed in the theater, I met Ralph, and you have already heard what a disaster that was." Somehow or other she wakened to the fact that she was sitting in Harry's lap and she felt very comfortable. Her head was leaning on his shoulder. "How did I get in this position? I don't remember moving at all."

"I'm glad, because I have something very private to tell you. Sukie said I should tell you how sorry I am for yelling at you. I think you are a marvelous mother and wife. Please believe me; I really mean this sincerely."

Laurie lifted her head, turned and looked at him with evident surprise.

"Why did Sukie have to tell you to apologize?"

"She helped show me what a fool I was," Harry confessed.

"Why did you yell at me and give me no time to answer?"

"I was a fool to listen to Ann's snide remarks. All I could see was you with very little on! I was jealous that others could see all that beauty when I felt you were all mine, especially after our wonderful afternoon together. I didn't even see that you were clearing Sean's lungs of water.''

He reached out and pulled the sleeve of her robe. His hand was teasing and caressing. His lips played with her mouth until her whole body throbbed. She melted into him to get closer and allowed his deeper entrance to her mouth. Lost in the vibration and sensations she was starved of, she didn't hear or see anything. She was mindless—only feeling. Laurie was hardly aware when Harry carried her upstairs.

Sun rays lit up the room and one bounced off a mirror into Laurie's eyes.

"Oh, my—is it morning already?" she moaned, and tried closing her eyes. "The best sleep I've had in a long time," she murmured, and turned over onto her back, clutching the blanket to stay in her nice comfortable nest. "I wonder how I got into bed last night? I don't—"

She sat up suddenly. "Harry?" Memory came flooding back. She looked over to his pillow and only his head imprint was there. Slowly lying back, she felt the way Scarlett did the morning after Rhett had spent the night with her. Laurie's eyes glowed as she wiggled her way sensuously back under the covers, pleased with the world and herself.

"This time was better than the last one," she said aloud, her eyes twinkling. "Oh, Harry, you did a very artful job of getting to me." She squirmed as sexuality started to take over. In the middle of her lustful daydream, the door opened and Harry entered, carrying a tray with breakfast on it, and two lovely red roses.

"Good morning, honey." He set the tray on a folding table he'd opened out. He sat on the side of the bed and lifted her to kiss her lightly. "Last night was memorable," he whispered delightfully in her ear.

Laurie whispered, ''Climb in and we'll try again. I'm not sure if you can better your performance.''

''Oh, yeah? You'll eat your breakfast first. Your strength needs building up if I'm to have my way with you. I've had my share of sausages, eggs with toast and coffee already, but I'll have another cup of coffee with you. Sit up so I can get the pillows arranged, or would you prefer to sit on the side of the bed?''

''I'll sit right here and pretend to be a lady of leisure.'' She started to drink her coffee and eat as soon as the tray was in front of her. ''Which reminds me. What's happened to Sukie and Maybelle and what time is it?''

Harry laughed and placed a kiss on her nose. ''First, it's almost noontime.''

''Oh, my word! Why didn't you wake me?''

''So I could have my way with you after you had rested well.'' Laurie giggled. ''We haven't seen or heard from Maybelle. I took Sukie over to the Harringtons'. She has gone to church with Todd, Neil and Sean and also has a luncheon invitation. She was eager to tell them all about yesterday's trip.''

''I hope she doesn't wear out their ears.'' She handed the tray over to him. ''That just hit the spot. I didn't realize how famished I was.''

''I've never heard Sukie chatter so much before coming here,'' he said, pushing the tray and table out of the way. He quickly leaned over to give her a hug and kiss, which deepened before he could catch his breath. She started pulling out his sweater and shirt from his jeans. Harry found himself trying to help her, pushing down her nightdress and prolonging his kiss at the same time.

He was half sprawled on the bed. One shoe was scraping off the other and he was trying to rid himself of a sock. And not getting anywhere with it. The other shoe came off and slid across the room. His arms and head got stuck in his sweater as Laurie tried pulling it off.

When he let go of her mouth, she pulled it over his head, bending his arms to get the sleeves off.

His face dropped into her lap and he continued kissing her all the way down. His lower half was arched and he fought to retain his balance. When he tried again to push his sock off, he slid down onto his knees. Laurie was trying to get him far enough up to undo his shirt buttons. When she realized she wasn't getting anywhere, she moved further down in the bed, reaching under him and groping for buttons. In frustration, she yanked, and the buttons snapped off, and she squealed, for Harry had reached her mound of Venus with his downward path of kisses. "Oh, love, don't stop," she groaned.

Harry gave up on the socks and unzipped his pants, and was trying to push them down when he fell off the bed, carrying her with him, as she was trying to get his shirtsleeves over his head and off his arms.

They rolled on the floor, giggling, as they finished removing his shirt. They melted into each other. When Harry finally came up for air, he discovered the middle of his back was hurting him. It dawned on him that something was wedged there. He rolled both himself and Laurie over, only to have her yell at him.

"Something is under me and it hurts!" He got up and helped raise her to her feet. "The bed will be a lot more comfortable and safer than this floor littered with shoes." She pushed the sheets and blankets back and climbed into bed, but she stopped him from getting in with her.

"Harry, hurry and get your pants off before you get into bed!"

The next hour kept them well occupied and then they dozed off, replenished and entangled with each other.

The next thing they knew the telephone rang-rang-rang, before Harry awoke enough to turn over to pick it up. "Um, that's me." Suddenly he sat up, alert and wide awake. "Please repeat what you have just said." He listened carefully and made a brief note on a pad of paper he kept close by the bed. "Yes, I'll be there as soon as I can be. Get some hot water ready for me, and towels ready on her bed. If the baby comes before I do, lay the baby in the towels after it cries, then place the baby on her abdomen and hold your wife's hand."

"Who's that?" Laurie sat up to see what was wrong. "Can I help?"

"Yes, if you can get dressed in ten minutes while I get my shoes on— Where are they?"

She got out of bed and, picking them up, tossed them to him. Then she raced to get into her underclothes and her jeans and sweatshirt and was downstairs in four minutes flat. She dashed to the car, struggling to get in her winter coat, and got it out of the barn and brought it to the door just as he ran down with his medical bag.

She slid over to let Harry drive, thinking he must know where he was going.

"You may have to help me. The cabin I am looking for is on Salomon's Creek, which runs down beside this road. We go about five miles on this road. On the right-hand side is a red letterbox at the foot of the road going up the hill. It makes it easier for the postman to see. Mrs. McLeod is expecting any moment now so help me keep a sharp eye out for it. As an afterthought, he told her, "She's having her first child."

The road was uphill and down and curved around the foothills.

"Why couldn't she get to the hospital?" Laurie asked.

"Mr. McLeod says his truck has broken down and when he called the hospital their two ambulances were out. So they told him to call me."

"Well, I'm glad we got one and a half good days in." She leaned over and patted his knee.

"Ah, here is the red box. I hope this car can make it on this narrow road. A good thing it's four-wheel drive.'' Calmly he negotiated the narrow switchback corners.

"Thank goodness I don't have to drive up this mountain. I'd be a nervous wreck by the time we got there,'' gasped Laurie.

"Relax. I think I saw some smoke in the air so we shouldn't have to go much further.''

"We're here,'' Laurie announced a couple of minutes later. She gave a big sigh of relief. "Mr. McLeod, we're here!'' she called as the door opened.

"Come in right now. I can see the baby's head. It's coming right now.''

"Bring me a small pan of hot water and we will take care of everything.'' Harry took off his coat as he strode in and threw it on a chair.

Mrs. McLeod was yelling for all she was worth. Laurie ran to her, grabbed her hands and held on tight.

"This child is ready to come, so take a deep breath and push when the next contraction comes.'' Harry was just in time to catch the boy.

"Here you are.'' Laurie handed him a towel which he laid the baby in.

"From the sound of him, he is going to lead you a merry chase.'' He finished his cleanup and put the boy in his father's arms.

Father and mother were admiring the fruits of their labor when a knock came at the door.

The door opened. "Yo-ho, I've arrived.''

"Well, Nurse Hart, about time—the excitement is all over. A nice, healthy-looking boy has arrived,'' Harry said.

"Hello, Mr. McLeod. I see they have put you to work. How are you feeling, Mrs. McLeod?''

"Just tired. We thank you good folks for coming to help us. Isn't he beautiful?''

On this note Harry and Laurie departed to try and finish their afternoon nap.

"That was the first time I've seen a baby born. It was a revelation. Thank you for asking me along." She reached out and gave him a hug then got in the car.

"While I do few birthings these days, I still find it an awesome experience, as Sukie would say. One of God's given miracles."

As they entered the house, Armand nearly tripped them up in her excitement to see them. Harry firmly picked her up, set her down in the kitchen and closed the door.

A banging on their door interrupted them just after they had climbed into bed to cuddle up.

"Who's there?" growled Harry. When there was no response, he asked again, "Who's there?"

"It's me, Maybelle."

"Oh, Mother, just a minute while we get dressed. Go to the kitchen and start some coffee, please."

"I'll start the coffee, but I also brought some champagne. Hurry up!" Maybelle insisted as her footsteps hurried down the stairs.

"What's she up to?" grunted Harry as he pushed himself out of bed to pull on his pants and shoes. His socks were still on. One look at his shirt and he went for another.

"Who knows? She hadn't come home when we came up. Had she?"

"I can't say. My mind was busy hauling you upstairs," he said, looking at her with a teasing glint in his eyes. "Don't gain any weight, 'cos I'm not getting any younger, you know. Once a day is all I can cope with."

CHAPTER TEN

"Mom, Dad, I'm home," Sukie called out as she slammed the door behind her. Faithful Armand greeted her with yips of pleasure. She tried to convey it all by jumping up to kiss her. Sukie patted her head and hugged her. "Hi, Maybelle," she said as she ran up, and pulled her down to kiss her. "Hi, Mr. Royce."

Hearing footsteps on the stairs, she ran over to meet her parents as they reached the floor. "Dad, Mom, I had an awesome time with Todd, Neil and Sean. After church, we all went to McDonald's and then their parents took us for a walk in the Unaka mountain range. Gee! There are a lot of trees up there, and water spouting out and over the rocks. It was cool. You'll have to go see it too, Dad."

"You bet; I'll go as soon as possible. Now that things have settled down in the hospital, Dr. Crinden and I will try to alternate weekends so we both have some time to spoil our families."

Laurie could see her mother was ready to explode. "What's up, Mother?"

"Emmett, would you please bring in the tray and champagne?" her mother asked.

Laurie started to question her as they wandered into the living room.

"No, dear—wait until Emmett comes back. We have an announcement to make."

When Emmett arrived she patted the table. "Put the tray right here, dear." The tray contained hors d'oeuvres and mini cupcakes with a droplet of whipped cream on top. A bottle of cold champagne and glasses were also on the tray. As soon as it was down she touched his arm and looked at him with the loveliest smile Laurie had ever seen on her mother's face.

"You make the announcement, dear."

"Ahem." He cleared his throat. "Maybelle and I have decided we suit each other and life is too short to waste. We need to enjoy life while we can— So I've asked her to marry me. She has honored me by accepting. We hope we have your approval."

"Mother!" Laurie threw herself at her and hugged her. "How wonderful! Oh, I'm so happy for you both!" Tears of happiness dropped from her eyes. "I had hoped this would happen. Oh, Mother, how delighted I am for both of you. I knew you were good friends at college and now—this is the frosting on the cake."

Harry handed her a handkerchief for each of them. The tears of happiness were washing their faces. Even Emmett dried up a tear or two while Harry shook his hand.

"We wish you everlasting contentment. Shall I break out the champagne for you?"

"Please do. I am so nervous I fear I will spray the house with it."

A glass of wine was handed to everyone, although Sukie's contained only one swallow.

"Here's to wedded bliss. You both deserve it." Harry raised his glass for the toast. They all drained their glasses. Laurie and Sukie then covered Emmett with kisses.

"We are so pleased you are joining our family," said Laurie. "When is this happy occasion going to take place?"

Sukie piped up before anyone could answer, "Can I be a bridesmaid?"

"You'll have to ask Maybelle first, but I have no objection," Emmett replied.

As soon as Maybelle stopped talking to her dad, Sukie went over and pulled on her sleeve. "Maybelle, can I be a bridesmaid?"

"You sure can, but I would rather have you as our flower girl."

"Oh, thank you, Maybelle." She reached up to kiss her. "You're the best grandma ever. Where are you going to live when you marry Mr. Royce?"

"About two blocks down the road from here. You can come see us when you can. I'll miss you too, dearest. I was so glad when you and your father came to live with us." Maybelle gave her another hug and kiss.

They celebrated until the champagne was finished. Harry made reservations in Johnson City and invited them to dinner.

"We would love to go," Maybelle said, giggling.

"What are your plans? How many people do you think will attend? Could we have the reception here at the house?" Harry spoke up and Laurie nodded in agreement.

"Let us have time to plan things. So far, we've been too excited to plan anything. We haven't told my brother, Arnold, and his family as yet." Emmett was looking smug and several years younger.

"We'll go and inform Arnold now. We'll meet you at the restaurant in one hour." Maybelle looked at Laurie to see if she agreed.

"That will be fine, Mother."

As soon as they were out of sight, Laurie stretched her arms in the air and flopped down in a chair. "This has been almost too exciting a day. Wouldn't you agree, dear?"

"This kind of pleasure makes my day."

"Daddy, what did you do that was so exciting?"

He gathered Sukie onto his lap. "Well, to begin the

day, I followed your advice and said I was sorry to Laurie, which made me very happy when she forgave me.''

"Oh, goody, Dad. See— I told you so.'' She gave him a kiss and then rushed to Laurie to give her a wet kiss also. "What else did you do?''

"Well, I made an emergency trip up into the hills to help deliver a boy child to a young couple. Their truck had broken down and they were stuck there.''

"What's his name?''

"Well, we left when Nurse Hart arrived and took over. They hadn't had time to name him. I needed to finish my weekend off from work. Then Grandma Maybelle and Emmett came with their wonderful news.''

"I'm going to be a flower girl and we're going out to dinner.'' She ran around, chanting in exuberance. "Just as if I was a grown-up.''

"Yes, and before we leave you need to take a shower because you won't have time when we return. Put on your new pink taffeta dress, as this is a special occasion. Also, lay out your clean clothes for school tomorrow and make sure your school pack is all together.'' Laurie directed her up the stairs and turned to see if Harry was coming.

"You go on up, honey. I'll follow as soon as I've checked a memo.''

He left for his den. In a quiet moment he gave thanks for the joy both Laurie and Sukie added to his life.

Laurie saw Sukie into her shower and picked out her favorite dress with all the petticoats for her and then went to pick out a special dress for herself to suit the occasion. She took three new dresses out of her closet, trying to decide which would be the better one. The green chiffon had a very low neckline and bare back. No, that one wouldn't do. She loved and was comfortable in the grey silk in the sweetheart style, but the floral print with the cowl neckline and full, flowing skirt seemed more appropriate for this special event.

How wonderful everything feels, Laura mused. Making up after our feud. To heck with the Ann Proctors of this world. He sure is one hunk of a man.

Wistfully she wondered if he would ever love her...

She was almost finished in the shower when the door opened and Harry stepped in.

"Need your back scrubbed?" he asked as his hands cupped her breasts. The vibrations and heat caught at her throat as she dissolved in ecstasy.

"That's not my back," Laurie replied as she turned to kiss him. "Let me wash you down. We don't have much time to fool around. Let's hurry."

A half-hour later, Laurie nudged Harry. "We have got to get dressed quickly if we are to arrive on time," she said as she rolled out of bed.

Sukie was ready and waiting for them. They were ten minutes late, but Maybelle and Emmett arrived right after them.

"Mother, Emmett, how did it go with Arnold?" Laurie asked as they sat at the table reserved for them.

"He and his daughters were very pleased. Joe wasn't there but I suspect he will vote along with them."

"How do you feel about your mother remarrying?" Emmett asked.

"I'm so delighted. It's a horrible feeling when families disagree," Laurie answered. "You know, I didn't realize there was such a nice first-class restaurant so close to us."

She turned and looked at the elegant room. The potted greenery was arranged so as to offer some privacy between tables. Dark blue tablecloths accented with a light pink tablecloth on top set off and matched the overall color scheme. Everything was clean and gleaming with polish. The chairs had castors so one could pull the chair in easily without having to lift it, and they were padded and covered with a dark blue velour material with flecks of assorted colors. Candles in crystal Aladdin's wishing lamps were glowing, giving the restaurant a cozy atmosphere.

"You did pick a lovely place to have our celebration dinner, and the funny thing is that when I first went out with Emmett he brought me here." Maybelle clasped his hand and, with stars in her eyes, gazed at him.

"Umm—this is a happy coincidence and makes the day for Laurie and me. We have squared away a misunderstanding." And Harry reached to clasp her hand.

Sukie, for once, was speechless. Her eyes were huge and she could hardly eat any of her dinner of hamburger and French fries. But, like all good things, it had to end. Even Cinderella had to leave the ball. On their arrival back at the house Harry carried his sleeping daughter inside and up to her bed.

"Darling, I'm bushed; bed looks so lovely," Laurie said once they were in their bedroom. "I don't know how you feel but everything was wonderful—nothing marred the day except that awful climb up and down that mountainside."

"Yes, it was a beautiful day. I hope the new addition to our world population is doing well. If I can find time, I will go up and check on the family."

"Let me know, because I would love to go with you. Even in spite of that crawl up the mountain."

"Hurry up, honey; tomorrow is Monday and back to work we go. You did say you were going in, didn't you?"

"Yes, and they told me I was to demonstrate a gall bladder attack."

"For once I am too tired to want anything but a close cuddle."

Laurie rolled over into his arms and was asleep before

Harry could count to ten. Her last thought was how secure she felt.

"I love you..." was the last whisper he heard.

Laurie had pushed and rushed Sukie to school. She was blurry-eyed and, for once, coffee hadn't helped to wake her a bit, she thought as she collapsed in the chair nearest the front door. "How do mothers survive growing children?" she said out loud.

Seeing the new young baby yesterday had been a thrill. Visions of a baby floated through her head as she checked her waist and rocked as if she were holding a child. The tears dropped one by one as she remembered her son, Dan, and the images she usually tried to blot out flooded into her mind.

Ralph had tossed a heavy, fur-lined coat, not caring where it landed. It had knocked Dan out and smothered him, and after Ralph had socked her he had left her out cold on the floor. She moaned and wept. How can I erase it from my mind? How long she remained there, tears falling freely, she didn't know—it seemed like a century. The next thing she knew, she was being lifted and placed on Harry's lap.

He held her close and murmured in a soothing tone of voice. She didn't hear what he said, but it calmed her down. Harry wiped her eyes and face with his handkerchief.

"What's wrong, honey?" he ventured.

"Oh, Harry, I was thinking about Sukie and seeing Robert McLeod, and wishing I was pregnant with your child, and then I remembered—" she sobbed "—about Danny. I couldn't stop crying. He was a beautiful baby. No doubt it was a mother's prejudice, but he was the most lovable boy. So happy—gurgling and smiling at me. I feel so guilty about not being able to save him. I was still unconscious when the police arrived. They took me to the hospital." The whole sad tale spewed out between her hiccups and sobs.

"Shh, shh, honey. It's all in the past. You will never

forget him but you need to forgive yourself. You were not responsible for his death—forgive yourself.''

She wiped her eyes and blew her nose. ''How come you're home now? Did the hospital burn down or something?'' She tried to joke.

''No, nothing so drastic. I just had a strong feeling I should come home and check on you. I don't know why, but I can see I came at the right time.''

''I'm not usually so weepy, but it just hit me and I couldn't stop.''

''You should have told me sooner. I know it's not your fault. You have to keep telling yourself you're not to blame until *you* believe it. I know you, and I know you would not hurt a child under any circumstances, especially your own.''

''I'll always mourn him.''

''You should remember him with joy for the pleasure you had together, not with guilt or regret.'' After a short pause he continued, ''What was his full name?''

''Daniel Patrick. I will try, dearest.'' She wiped her eyes with his damp handkerchief.

''That's my girl! Have you had breakfast yet?''

''No, I wasn't too hungry, and I had a heck of a time getting Sukie off to school. She was slower than molasses for some reason.''

''I hope this isn't a sign that she's coming down with something. You have a list of all the ailments she's had and all her shot records, haven't you?'' Laurie nodded. Harry got up and stood her on her feet then led her into the kitchen.

''I think a good dish of oatmeal and a glass of orange juice would just hit the spot. If you're asking my preference.'' Laurie sat down.

''Now you know I don't know how to make that nasty stuff,'' he said as he started looking in the fridge for the orange juice.

''Well, it's very simple. Take my extra-large glass

measuring cup and fill it with one cup of water. Use one scoop of oatmeal, add a tablespoon of cut-up dates, out of the canning jar next to it, then salt and place it in the microwave. Set the timer for five minutes on high temperature.''

"I thought you cooked in a pan when you made it before."

"I did; the pan holds more and I have to stir it constantly to prevent it from burning on the bottom. This other way prevents burning and I don't have to stir all the time."

"OK. We'll make it your way. Afterwards, I need to get back as I've delayed an operation to come here."

"That will be fine, Harry. Don't worry, I'll be back in full swing as soon as I eat. Delia will be here before long. We had planned to clean out some of the attic. It's still dirty from when the men reroofed the house."

"Don't work too hard, love." He stood her up, hugged and kissed her. "You and Sukie are the only things that matter to me."

That evening, Laurie's mother and her prospective groom arrived to inform them of their plans.

"We are so excited, it was hard to decide. We both have lots of friends but we decided we would really prefer having a small wedding with just immediate family, this being a second marriage for us both."

"We have already talked with the minister and as soon as we apply for our license we will arrange the date," stated Emmett.

"That sounds great. So can we have the reception here for you, Mother?"

"I think it's a delightful idea. There is only Arnold with his two girls, one married, and a son. That makes five, and then us—ten in total. And would you mind if Emmett and I each invited two or three special friends to join us here at the house?" Maybelle queried.

"You know we wouldn't." Laurie glanced at her husband who was nodding in agreement.

Emmett cleared his throat. "I would like to contribute a case of champagne and Hetti, my housekeeper and cook, would love to help out with the preparing of the feast."

"That's a great idea!" Harry exclaimed. "I was wondering if my wife wasn't taking on too much. Now all we need is a waitress and a bartender."

"Mother, what time of the day are you planning this ceremony?" Laurie rose from her chair and headed for the kitchen. "I know a perfect couple, if it is during the day. Hold everything while I bring some tea and coffee for us—or would you prefer something else?"

"No, I would like a cup of tea," Maybelle said. "What do you men say?"

"The two men agreed that that would be fine.

The tea and coffee were served with cookies and a hot chocolate had been made for Sukie; she had finished her homework and, hearing the familiar voices, had quickly come downstairs. Now she sat and listened carefully to all the plans.

"We've planned to go to Niagara Falls in Canada for our honeymoon. After checking plane schedules, we found we can take a flight in a friend's plane to Atlanta, Georgia and the flight to Canada leaves around two-thirty in the afternoon for Toronto." Maybelle stopped and sipped her tea.

Emmett took over. "We hope to arrange for the service to be Friday morning at nine a.m. so we can leave about eleven-thirty for our flight from Tricity Airport."

"It sounds splendid. That leaves us a few days to get everything ready. Mother, after you leave, would you like Hetti and me to pack your things and take them to your new home?"

"Thanks; I was wondering how I could handle everything before I left."

Emmett spoke up. "Harry, when we get back from our honeymoon, why don't you arrange to take one for you and Laurie? We know you didn't have time before, and we can take care of Sukie while you're away."

"I would love to take you up on the offer, but as the new administrator of the hospital and with only two surgeons available it may be difficult—especially as I've only been here such a short time. But I'll keep it in mind and let you know."

Friday turned out to be a beautiful day for a wedding. Refreshingly cool and invigorating. The sun shines on the bride today, Laurie thought with pleasure.

They all arrived at the church on time and Sukie skipped in front of Laurie and the bride, tossing her rose petals for them to walk on. Harry stood as best man, waiting with Emmett at the front, near the minister.

As he watched his family walk up the aisle, faces full of joy, Harry felt he had done them wrong when he'd married Laurie in such a slam-bang hurry. Sukie had also been cheated out of the pleasure of standing with them. What a fool I have been, he thought. I can mend broken bodies but not broken dreams. I may have to take a lesson from these two.

Laurie walked on the rose petals and, seeing Sukie's happy face, felt the loss of her daydreams. At her daughter's age, she'd dreamed of fairy princesses in castles, with a prince on a white charger to rescue her from the wicked stepmother.

She grinned to herself. The prince really did save my home and he is good in bed, she thought. If he only loved me, I would be truly happy. I may at times be a wicked stepmother. Who knows? Mother looks so happy; I am proud she has the courage to move on in her life. Thanks again to my knight. A pity he doesn't ride a white horse, only in a sleek black car.

Harry had to leave right after the ceremony as he had

a backlog of patients waiting. He kissed the new Mrs. Royce and shook hands with Mr. Royce, wishing them joy and good health in their new adventure. Their friends and family showered them with best wishes, and confetti. Sukie, with more rose petals, sat on Arnold's shoulders and tried to cover them with roses of all colors.

Back at the house, the sandwiches and drinks vanished quickly, then the couple cut the wedding cake, and Hetti, Emmett's cook, helped finish the cutting and parceled the slices out.

An hour later, all the guests left after eating their fill and talking up a storm. As the last one departed, Laurie, Delia and Hetti all collapsed and gave a sigh of relief.

"Well, that's done and over. Now what?" Sukie piped up.

"First thing is to let me take one more picture of you in the garden." As soon as the picture was taken, they returned indoors. "Now you need to take off your lovely dress and put on play-clothes."

"Aw, I want to show Polina, Lou Ellen and the boys. The boys won't believe that I looked so fine in my special dress."

Laurie shook her head and tried to remember how it was at that age. "Well, love, you have a choice. You can either go show them your lovely dress when school is out and take a chance that you don't get it dirty or ripped. Or you put on your jeans so you can play and show them the pictures of you all dressed up later. You look lovely but the choice is yours."

"If I take it off before it gets too dirty, can I wear it to church Sunday?"

"Yes, dear. Hang it up and I will check it for spots when I come upstairs. Now I need to help clean up. Maybe when you're changed and waiting for school to let out you can help straighten out the living room and dining room."

Sukie skipped up the stairs and Armand, having been let loose from her dog house, followed in her footsteps.

Harry wasn't able to go with them the following week to see *Over-mountain Men* play at the high school as he was tied up with a last-minute emergency appendicitis case. Mr. and Mrs. Royce had given their tickets to Arnold, who brought Marion, his daughter. They went in his car to the school auditorium.

"I didn't sell but twenty-four tickets," Sukie moaned in disgust.

"Hey, not to worry, Sukie. You did better than I did when I tried to sell tickets to the same play. I only sold four to my dad, after going from door to door. Twenty-four tickets is nothing to sneeze at," Laurie encouraged her. "In my day, all anyone ever averaged was eight or so. You did very well, dear."

The play was very well done and, having gone to Rocky Mount, Sukie was able to understand the struggle it had been for the settlers to climb the Gaps and cut their way through the wild brush and trees on the ranges which made up parts of the Appalachian Mountains. The settlers had found patches of flat or sloping valley floors to build their log cabins, they sowed their crops and discovered the wild fruits they could pick. They admired from a distance the rhododendrons' blaze of color, but did not appreciate the chopping it took to try and make a path through them. Hunting was plentiful for them.

The play highlighted the human trials and struggles to survive. Sukie was enthralled and decided right then and there she would try for a part in the next play. The end came too soon for her.

They got home shortly after ten-thirty and Laurie helped her daughter get into bed. Sukie was out like a light.

Harry was home reading and had made a cup of hot chocolate for each of them. They relaxed while drinking and discussed their day before going upstairs, arms around each other's waist.

Harry left the next morning before Laurie awakened. Oh, what was the matter with her? she wondered. She had overslept and, while there was no school today, she liked to make Sukie a special breakfast on the weekends. It was an effort to get out of bed. She was light-headed and she felt queasy. I hope I'm not coming down with the flu, she thought as she dragged her clothes on and fumbled her way downstairs.

"Dad said not to wake you. So I made hot chocolate in the microwave." Sukie looked up from the pamphlet she was reading. It was about the life of Nancy Ward, a Cherokee chieftain; her mom had gotten it for her.

"Thanks, love." She flopped down in a chair and propped her head in her hands.

"What's wrong, Mom? You look sick."

"I hope I'm not coming down with the flu. Could you please get your own breakfast today? Even the smell of coffee turns me off." She got up and went to lie down on the living-room couch. She was asleep again almost before she laid her head down.

Sukie came in and stared at her. She covered her with the blanket kept for that purpose. Laurie had never acted like this before. I don't want to call Dad, she thought, but maybe Delia would come and help me before I call him?

She picked up the phone. "Delia, my mother looks as if she is coming down with the flu," she said when the housekeeper answered. "She said coffee made her sick and she is on the couch and asleep. Dad says not to call him unless it's a real emergency."

"Hang up, Sukie; I'll be there in about ten minutes."

"Thanks, Delia." As she hung up she gave a sigh of relief and felt a lot better. She got herself a bowl of cereal with strawberries she found in the fridge. She ate while she waited for Delia.

"Miss Laurie, are you feeling all right? I felt your head and you're not hot with fever," Delia said some minutes later, out of breath from hurrying.

Laurie stretched and slowly sat up. "I guess I'm tired out from all the excitement we've had."

"How about some coffee now? I'll bring you some," she said, and she departed for the kitchen to fetch it.

"Oh, Delia, that smells awful. Please take it away," Laurie protested when Delia returned, and she lay back down and covered her eyes.

Delia laughed and then caught sight of a frightened Sukie. "Why don't you take this coffee into the kitchen, dear? I don't think there is anything really wrong. How about going upstairs afterwards and cleaning your room and making up your bed? I'll stay with your mom while you're gone."

"OK, Delia." Sukie went reluctantly up the stairs, looking back as if she wasn't sure if she could believe her.

"Now that big ears is upstairs, we'll talk. Has this feeling bad in the morning been happening other mornings? Are you finding yourself sleepy all the time?"

"Yeah." She looked surprisingly pleased. "Delia, do you really think so?"

"Well, there is one way to prove it. I have a test kit at home and Buddy can run it up in a few minutes."

"Oh, Delia, you are an angel." Laurie rose and hugged her.

"OK, let me get this phone call through."

Half an hour later, Laurie danced out of the washroom. "It's positive!" Grabbing hold of Sukie, who had just come downstairs, she whirled her around. "I'm not sick and have good news for your dad—I hope for you too, but it will have to wait until I tell him first."

"I bet I know. Polina's mother has been having what she calls morning sickness each day. She is going to have a baby. Are you going to have one?"

"I hope so." Watching Sukie carefully, Laurie asked, "Would it upset you to have a sister or brother?"

"I don't know for sure. My friends' sisters and brothers can be a real nuisance—fighting and calling each other names, and taking each other's toys. But I guess I could like one." She said wistfully, "I used to think I wanted a sister, but Dad always said it wasn't possible."

"Well, I believe this is very possible, but it's kind of early to say definitely. So we don't want to tell anyone right away, except Dad. When it's safe, then you can tell everyone. Think you can wait?"

"I'll try. Delia knows...can Grandma know?"

"Yes, we'll tell her when she's home."

"Goody. Can I go see if Neil will play with me?"

"Sure, but no loose lips, please. I take it your room is picked up?"

"Yeah." Sukie ran out the back door and down the hill with blonde hair flying.

"Well," said Delia, "now that we know it's not the flu, get yourself some breakfast. Tea and crackers first. I've got to get back and make sure those lazy boys of mine don't sneak out before doing their chores."

"Thanks, Delia; this goes beyond the call of duty." Laurie hugged her and kissed her cheek.

"Go on with you! What are friends for?"

The following day, Laurie almost overslept again, but the tea and crackers that Sukie brought up helped her upset stomach. Oh, dear! she thought. How will this affect our contract? He will surely make this a permanent marriage...won't he? Oh, dear! What can I do now? First, I'm not going to tell him until I have to.

Harry was busy in his den, working. When asked if he would go to church with them he declined as he was on call for emergencies. He had his beeper, but having to leave in the middle of a prayer or sermon wasn't for him. When they returned, he was still there, and had decided to take them out to lunch locally. His beeper went off just as he ordered dessert and coffee, and he left them as soon as he'd spoken to the hospital on the telephone. A movie seemed like a good thing to do before going home to an empty house.

A week passed and Harry was so busy that they saw little of him. But the weekend coming was his weekend off. Maybe she could find time to talk to him then.

Saturday morning, Harry woke and, deciding to leave Laurie sleeping for a while longer, went to see if Sukie was up. They could make their own breakfast, eat and then wake Laurie. He needed time alone with his daughter.

"Hi, dad; I beat you down today. Is Laurie coming down?"

"Not yet. I thought I would let her sleep until we're finished down here."

"Yeah, she needs her sleep," she said, surprising her father with her concern.

"Let's make breakfast, eat, and then we can take hers on a tray and wake her."

Now how am I going to get Mom's tea and crackers up to her? Sukie wondered. With Dad so busy, she hasn't found time to tell him the news. Sukie thought hard, but no answers came up. As they ate her dad asked her questions.

"How's school going? Are your grades holding up?" He spoke between bites of toast, scrambled eggs and sausage.

"I've gotten good marks. Miss Clemons says she is pleased with me. On all my exams I had an A or B."

"That sounds great, dear. Are you happy here?"

"A lot better than when I had baby-sitters. Some of them were fun, but I have more chances to play outside here. My friends are nice. I love Mom and Maybelle. They make me feel good. How about you, Dad?"

"I love my work, Laurie is a marvelous wife and

Maybelle makes a great grandmother. I have a happy, lovely daughter that I am proud of. Life couldn't be better.''

Sukie went and climbed into her father's lap and gave him a kiss and hug. "I love you, Daddy.''

He held her for a while, smoothing her hair. "I'm so lucky to have such a loving, beautiful daughter. I love you too.''

"Come on, let's fix Mom's breakfast,'' Sukie said, and jumped off her father's lap. Oh, and before I forget, Mom has decided to switch to tea. It has less caffeine.''

He looked at her in surprise as he rose from his chair. "When did all this come about? She normally needs two cups of coffee to wake up.''

"Well, she told me that she read in a medical magazine how bad caffeine is for you. She decided to change to tea because she couldn't stand the smell of decaffeinated coffee.''

Her dad seemed to accept her story. Now to get the crackers up without him seeing. While his back was turned, she slipped some out of the can. Hiding them behind her, she sneaked up the stairs.

Harry heard the stairs squeak and looked around. No Sukie... Hmm, I wonder what she's up to now? he thought.

He carried the tray into their bedroom, following Sukie. Setting the tray down, he leaned over to kiss her awake. "Wake up, Sleeping Beauty.'' He kissed her on her straight, aristocratic nose. "Rise and shine, beloved. It's breakfast-time.''

"Mom, Dad has brought you your tea and here are your favorite crackers,'' Sukie said as she handed them to Laurie. "I'll put your cup of tea right beside you on your nightstand.''

"Thanks, doll.'' Laurie started to nibble on her crackers without opening her eyes.

Harry watched his daughter's rush to help in astonishment. Now what are they up to? he wondered. When the crackers were finished, Laurie didn't sit up but sipped her tea through a drinking straw Sukie had added to the cup, which she held for her mother.

Harry, you poor, stupid sod, get out of here a moment and let your daughter do what she has obviously been doing for a while. He departed to the bathroom to think. Why hasn't she told me? he wondered. He started grinning. I'm to be a father again. Well, I will have to wait a while. She can't keep it a secret for too long. But Sukie must know, otherwise how would she know about crackers and tea?

He washed his hands and flushed the toilet after peeking to see if the tea was down. He heard Sukie whispering. Ah! he thought. She is getting ready to sit up. I'd better get out in case plans don't work out.

"All set to eat now?"

"Darling, I didn't realize you'd come up," she said, adding weakly, "Yes, I'm ready for breakfast."

"Well, it's kind of gotten cold by now, so I'll heat it up and return," he said diplomatically, and, picking up the tray, he moved out and returned in a short while.

"Here's some hot oatmeal just as you like." He placed it in front of her on the tray. She looked a little less green.

The rest of the day, they drove around the country lanes, admiring some of the dammed rivers that created boat and fishing areas, and helped feed the Tennessee River with hydroelectric power. It was a peaceful day. Harry had a smirk on his face. Laurie was just content, but she wondered when and where she would tell him about the baby.

Later, after supper, Harry took his wife for a short walk around the grounds to see how the animals and orchards were faring under Delia's husband's care.

"It's so pleasant out here. Oh, Harry, I do so love

you. I think I'd better tell you that I am expecting our child in about eight months.'' She blurted it out in a rush of breath, not sure how he would take it.

"I wondered when you were going to get around to telling me. I know it's hard to find time for us to even talk, but you took your time. Even Sukie knew before I did. I'll forgive you, though. My one and only, loving you has become my dearest joy.'' Passion swept them into a loving embrace with a kiss that was deep, fiery and endless.

Sukie and Delia watched from the kitchen. "Why is he doing CPR Delia?"

"Honey, you are a bit young for a peeping Thomasina.''

"I'm not peeping, I just need to know medical techniques.'' She looked at Delia.

A skeptical Delia said, "He sure ain't using medically approved CPR. He's just kissing her. Honey, when you are their age, it will surely get your heart pumping away too.''

"Oh? Oh!''

EPILOGUE

"CHRISTMAS EVE is such a wonderful time of the year." Laurie huddled up to Harry as they walked out of the church. He helped Sukie keep up and Maybelle and Emmett followed behind.

"The service was great and they played my favorite tunes," Maybelle remarked. "The boys' choir surpassed themselves in their singing of, 'It Came Upon a Midnight Clear'. Neil Harrington has a marvelous soprano voice."

"Why is it all those angelic voices are generally such rascals?" Laurie laughed.

Halfway up the hill, Sukie started stumbling. She was having a difficult time staying awake. Harry swept her up into his arms. Her face nestled into his neck. "I love you, Dad," she said as she relaxed and became a dead weight. He was out of breath after climbing up the rest of the hill and up the stairs with Sukie.

Having left the Royces at their home, Laurie entered the house behind Harry. She locked the doors and went to help put Sukie to bed. They undressed her to her panties and her slip and slid her under the blankets.

"Wait a moment and I'll get her stocking out of our dirty-clothes hamper. It's wrapped in a sheet and a plastic bag." Laurie hurried to her task, giggling all the way. "Sukie has been sneaking up here and looking everywhere," she whispered as she hung the stocking at the foot of her bed. "Let's hurry up and put the gifts under the tree."

"Hurry up, love; let's get this over with so we can get at least two hours of sleep." Harry pulled her down the hall and stairs and rushed to his den and unlocked the door. The packages had all been stored in there to keep Sukie and other nosy people out.

The fun of their first Christmas together was an exciting event for them. Everything was placed under the tree, including Sukie's new sled, and a doll with a fancy Southern Belle dress made by Maybelle. It had pantaloons, a corset, a chemise, one petticoat with a wire through the hem to hold it out and another with fancy lace ruffles topped by a red velvet dress.

While Laurie was admiring the twinkle of the ornaments on the tree, Harry rushed to the kitchen, and came out with two glasses filled with eggnog, made the old-fashioned southern way. Harry had gotten Maybelle to help him make it. It really was something! he'd thought when he had tasted it before.

"Here's to the loveliest Southern Belle with all my heart."

"Oh, Harry, you are a prime piece of manhood." She sipped her drink. "Whoo! Who made this? It's a smooth eggnog."

"With Maybelle's instructions, I made it. It's good. Let's put our drinks on the table for a moment. Since it's past midnight, here is a token of my affection." He dug out an envelope from his hip pocket and handed it to Laurie.

What can it be? she thought as she ripped the envelope open. Inside was the ninety-day contract she'd signed. Her heart dropped as she looked at it. Could he have decided to end it, or did he want her to end it? Her stricken eyes looked up at him. "Is this supposed to be a message to me?"

"My love, your eyes have given me my answer. The only thing this signifies is that the ninety days are up and I hope and pray that the love I have for you and which I hope you have for me will make you want to tear up the contract and make this a very *real* marriage. Especially now that you are carrying our child.''

She let out a burst of air as she tried to pump more into her lungs. ''Oh, Harry—of course I love you! You're my husband, my other half. I...'' She stopped, decisively, and ripped the contract up and laid it on the table.

''Oh, Laurie...'' Harry gathered her up into his arms and covered her in kisses. ''Good...that's settled!'' he said at last. ''You love me and I love you.''

''There is one thing... What about my option to renew for a four-year period?'' Laurie teased lightly, secure in Harry's embrace.

''Well, you could say I want to renew it further... What are you doing for the next sixty or so years?''

Laurie laughed and kissed him in response. It was all the answer he needed.

EVER HAD ONE OF THOSE DAYS?

TO DO:

☑ late for a super-important meeting, you discover the cat has eaten your panty hose

☑ while you work through lunch, the rest of the gang goes out and finds a one-hour, once-in-a-lifetime 90% off sale at the most exclusive store in town (Oh, and they also get to meet Brad Pitt who's filming a movie across the street.)

☑ you discover that your intimate phone call with your boyfriend was on company-wide intercom

☑ finally at the end of a long and exasperating day, you escape from it all with an entertaining, humorous and always romantic Love & Laughter book!

ENJOY
LOVE & LAUGHTER™
EVERY DAY!

For a preview, turn the page....

Here's a sneak peek at
Colleen Collins's RIGHT CHEST, WRONG NAME
Available August 1997...

———————

"DARLING, YOU SOUND like a broken cappuccino machine," murmured Charlotte, her voice oozing disapproval.

Russell juggled the receiver while attempting to sit up in bed, but couldn't. If he *sounded* like a wreck over the phone, he could only imagine what he looked like.

"What mischief did you and your friends get into at your bachelor's party last night?" she continued.

She always had a way of saying "your friends" as though they were a pack of degenerate water buffalo. Professors deserved to be several notches higher up on the food chain, he thought. Which he would have said if his tongue wasn't swollen to twice its size.

"You didn't do anything...bad...did you, Russell?"

"Bad." His laugh came out like a bark.

"Bad as in *naughty.*"

He heard her piqued tone but knew she'd never admit to such a base emotion as jealousy. Charlotte Maday, the woman he was to wed in a week, came from a family who bled blue. Exhibiting raw emotion was akin to burping in public.

After agreeing to be at her parents' pool party by

noon, he untangled himself from the bed sheets and stumbled to the bathroom.

"Pool party," he reminded himself. He'd put on his best front and accommodate Char's request. Make the family rounds, exchange a few pleasantries, play the role she liked best: the erudite, cultured English literature professor. After fulfilling his duties, he'd slink into some lawn chair, preferably one in the shade, and nurse his hangover.

He tossed back a few aspirin and splashed cold water on his face. Grappling for a towel, he squinted into the mirror.

Then he jerked upright and stared at his reflection, blinking back drops of water. "Good Lord. They stuck me in a wind tunnel."

His hair, usually neatly parted and combed, sprang from his head as though he'd been struck by lightning. "Can too many Wild Turkeys do that?" he asked himself as he stared with horror at his reflection.

Something caught his eye in the mirror. Russell's gaze dropped.

"What in the—"

Over his pectoral muscle was a small patch of white. A bandage. Gingerly, he pulled it off.

Underneath, on his skin, was not a wound but a small, neat drawing.

"A red heart?" His voice cracked on the word *heart*. Something—a word?—was scrawled across it.

"Good Lord," he croaked. "I got a tattoo. A heart tattoo with the name Liz on it."

Not Charlotte. Liz!

Coming in August 1997!

THE BETTY NEELS
RUBY COLLECTION

COLLECTOR'S EDITION

This August start assembling the
Betty Neels Ruby Collection. Six of the
most requested and best-loved titles have
been especially chosen for this collection.
From August 1997 until January 1998,
one title per month will be available to avid
fans. Spot the collection by the lush ruby red
cover with the gold Collector's Edition banner
and your favorite author's name—Betty Neels!

Available in August at your favorite retail outlet.

HARLEQUIN®

Take 4 bestselling love stories FREE

Plus get a FREE surprise gift!

Don't miss these Harlequin favorites by some of our most popular authors! And now you can receive a discount by ordering two or more titles!

HT#25700	HOLDING OUT FOR A HERO		
	by Vicki Lewis Thompson	$3.50 U.S. ☐/$3.99 CAN. ☐
HT#25699	WICKED WAYS		
	by Kate Hoffmann	$3.50 U.S. ☐/$3.99 CAN. ☐
HP#11845	RELATIVE SINS		
	by Anne Mather	$3.50 U.S. ☐/$3.99 CAN. ☐
HP#11849	A KISS TO REMEMBER		
	by Miranda Lee	$3.50 U.S. ☐/$3.99 CAN. ☐
HR#03359	FAITH, HOPE AND MARRIAGE		
	by Emma Goldrick	$2.99 U.S. ☐/$3.50 CAN. ☐
HR#03433	TEMPORARY HUSBAND		
	by Day Leclaire	$3.25 U.S. ☐/$3.75 CAN. ☐
HS#70679	QUEEN OF THE DIXIE DRIVE-IN		
	by Peg Sutherland	$3.99 U.S. ☐/$4.50 CAN. ☐
HS#70712	SUGAR BABY		
	by Karen Young	$3.99 U.S. ☐/$4.50 CAN. ☐
HI#22319	BREATHLESS		
	by Carly Bishop	$3.50 U.S. ☐/$3.99 CAN. ☐
HI#22335	BEAUTY VS. THE BEAST		
	by M.J. Rodgers	$3.50 U.S. ☐/$3.99 CAN. ☐
AR#16577	BRIDE OF THE BADLANDS		
	by Jule McBride	$3.50 U.S. ☐/$3.99 CAN. ☐
AR#16656	RED-HOT RANCHMAN		
	by Victoria Pade	$3.75 U.S. ☐/$4.25 CAN. ☐
HH#28868	THE SAXON		
	by Margaret Moore	$4.50 U.S. ☐/$4.99 CAN. ☐
HH#28893	UNICORN VENGEANCE		
	by Claire Delacroix	$4.50 U.S. ☐/$4.99 CAN. ☐

(limited quantities available on certain titles)

	TOTAL AMOUNT	$ _____
DEDUCT:	**10% DISCOUNT FOR 2+ BOOKS**	$ _____
	POSTAGE & HANDLING	$ _____
	($1.00 for one book, 50¢ for each additional)	
	APPLICABLE TAXES*	$ _____
	TOTAL PAYABLE	$ _____
	(check or money order—please do not send cash)	

To order, complete this form, along with a check or money order for the total above, payable to Harlequin Books, to: **In the U.S.:** 3010 Walden Avenue, P.O. Box 9047, Buffalo, NY 14269-9047; **In Canada:** P.O. Box 613, Fort Erie, Ontario, L2A 5X3.

Name: _____

Address: _____ City: _____

State/Prov.: _____ Zip/Postal Code: _____

*New York residents remit applicable sales taxes.
Canadian residents remit applicable GST and provincial taxes.

Look us up on-line at: http://www.romance.net

HBKJS97

As Seen on TV!

Free Gift Offer

With a Free Gift proof-of-purchase
from any Harlequin® book, you can receive
a beautiful cubic zirconia pendant.

This stunning marquise-shaped stone is a genuine cubic
zirconia—accented by an 18" gold tone necklace.
(Approximate retail value $19.95)

Send for yours today...
compliments of ◆HARLEQUIN®

To receive your free gift, a cubic zirconia pendant, send us one original proof-of-purchase, photocopies not accepted, from the back of any Harlequin Romance®, Harlequin Presents®, Harlequin Temptation®, Harlequin Superromance®, Harlequin Intrigue®, Harlequin American Romance®, or Harlequin Historicals® title available at your favorite retail outlet, together with the Free Gift Certificate, plus a check or money order for $1.65 U.S./$2.15 CAN. (do not send cash) to cover postage and handling, payable to Harlequin Free Gift Offer. We will send you the specified gift. Allow 6 to 8 weeks for delivery. Offer good until December 31, 1997, or while quantities last. Offer valid in the U.S. and Canada only.

Free Gift Certificate

Name: _____

Address: _____

City: _____ State/Province: _____ Zip/Postal Code: _____

Mail this certificate, one proof-of-purchase and a check or money order for postage and handling to: HARLEQUIN FREE GIFT OFFER 1997. In the U.S.: 3010 Walden Avenue, P.O. Box 9071, Buffalo NY 14269-9057. In Canada: P.O. Box 604, Fort Erie, Ontario L2Z 5X3.

FREE GIFT OFFER   084-KEZ

ONE PROOF-OF-PURCHASE

To collect your fabulous FREE GIFT, a cubic zirconia pendant, you must include this
original proof-of-purchase for each gift with the properly completed Free Gift Certificate.

084-KEZR